Laura and I were old friends. She was about two years older than I, a very handsome, fine-looking girl. We had always been on very good terms as children, but she had a sort of haughty, imperious air which, joined to the difference in our ages, had operated in a manner that would have prevented me from thinking of taking any liberties with her . . .

When I again met her, I found that a considerable change had taken place in her person. I too had grown considerably during this period . . . Altogether, I could not help acknowledging to myself that I had rarely seen a handsomer or finer-looking woman.

LAURA MIDDLETON
and
THE NEW EPICUREAN

Anonymous

NEXUS
published by
the Paperback Division of
W.H. ALLEN & Co. PLC

A Nexus Book
Published in 1984
by the Paperback Division of
W. H. Allen & Co. Plc
Sekforde House, 175/9 St. John Street,
London, EC1V 4LL

Reprinted 1985, 1989

Typeset by Phoenix Photosetting, Chatham

Printed and bound in Great Britain by
Courier International Ltd, Tiptree, Essex

ISBN 0 352 31530 X

LAURA MIDDLETON

HER BROTHER
and
HER LOVER

The remarks which Emily had made regarding the share Laura Middleton had had in opening up her ideas on the subject to the mysteries in which she had now been fully initiated had not escaped my observation. It so happened that at that very time I was under an engagement to pay a visit to the Middletons, who were very distant relations of my mother. It of course occurred to me that it was possible I might be able to turn the information I had thus acquired to some account. Laura and I were old friends. She was about two years older than I, a very handsome, fine-looking girl but, as I had then fancied, upon rather a larger scale than quite suited my taste. We had always been on very good terms as children, but she had a sort of haughty, imperious air which, joined to the difference in our ages, had operated in a manner that would have prevented me from thinking of taking any liberties with her; and she was about the last person in the world I should have been disposed to imagine addicted to the amusements in which Emily had participated with her.

When I again met her on arriving at their country seat, I found that a considerable change had taken place in her person, but probably this was merely the natural result that the preceding two years, during which I had not seen her, had worked upon a girl at her time of life, by fully developing the proportions and fining down the parts of the figure which at an earlier period might have appeared too prominent. I too had grown considerably during this period, more so in proportion than she had, and now her height by no means appeared to me to be too great; and altogether, I could not help acknowledging to myself that I had rarely seen a handsomer or finer-looking woman. She still retained somewhat of her haughty air, though softened down, and I could hardly fancy, when looking at her, that Emily's account of her behaviour in the hours when she gave herself up to enjoyment could be true. I soon, however, became aware of circumstances that tended to corroborate that tale, and which put me in the way of making advances to her, which I hastened to do.

When it came to be time to dress for dinner, Lady Middleton said to me that she had presumed on our relationship to put me into the family wing of the house, as the arrival of some unexpected visitors had made her change the destination of the room she had previously intended for me. She said no doubt I would find the one set apart for me quite comfortable, for the only objection to it, and which prevented her from being able to put a stranger into it, was that it opened into another room which would have to be occupied by her son Frank, who was expected home from school in a short time. This last room, in consequence of some alterations made in building an addition to the house, had no separate entrance, but opened into the two rooms on each side, and as the one on the other side was occupied by his sister and aunt, Frank would have to enter through mine. She said I must keep him in order and make him behave himself, and if I had any trouble with him to let her know. I had not seen my young namesake for about two years, but I recollected him as a fine, high-spirited, very handsome boy always getting into some scrape or other and always getting out of them somehow in such a fearless, good-humoured manner that it was impossible for anyone to be angry with

4

him. So I said I should be delighted to renew my acquaintance with my young friend, and that I had not the least doubt but that we should get on very pleasantly.

On going to my room to dress for dinner, I found a servant-girl engaged in making some of the arrangements which the change of apartments had necessitated. On my entrance she was going to leave the room, but seeing that she was a very nice-looking young girl, I said she need not run away in such a hurry, that surely she was not afraid of me. She gave me an arch look as if taking the measure of my capacities, and replied with a smile that she did not think she need be afraid of such a nice-looking young gentleman. This I thought was a fair challenge, and it induced me to take a better look at her. I found she was a very well made country girl of about nineteen, with some very promising points about her. I therefore kept her in conversation for a short time, while I went on with my washing operation. Finding she was in no hurry to leave me, I went up to her as she was engaged in putting the bed in order and snatched a few kisses. I then commenced playing with her bubbies and taking some further liberties with her. As my proceedings met with very little resistance, beyond a few exclamations of 'Oh for shame, I did not expect such conduct from you,' I proceeded with my researches and without much difficulty I succeeded in raising her petticoats and getting possession of her stronghold. On insinuating my finger within it, I found it to be tighter and even more inviting than I had anticipated.

She soon became excited with my caresses and the titillation which my finger kept up without her fortress, and I succeeded in laying her upon the bed and throwing up her clothes so as to disclose it fairly to my view. I found a fine, fresh white belly and a pair of plump, handsome thighs with a very pretty little opening tolerably well shaded with light brown hair. Altogether it was a very desirable prospect, and I thought that failing anything better I might manage to find a good deal of enjoyment in her charms. Slipping off my

5

trousers, therefore, I jumped up beside her on the bed, and throwing my arms round her, I got upon her and attempted to introduce myself into the fortress. But here I found greater resistance than I had anticipated from her previous conduct.

I had observed, however, the effect my caresses had produced on her senses. I thought the best plan would be to endeavour to excite them still more. So, insinuating the finger of one hand again into the critical spot, and with the other drawing my shirt over my head so as to leave myself entirely naked, I raised myself on my knees beside her, exhibiting my standard fully erected, flaming fiercely before her eyes. While continuing to excite her by the movements of my finger, I said I was sure she would not be cruel enough to refuse me, but would take pity upon the little suppliant that was begging so hard for admittance. Taking hold of her hand I placed it upon the stiff object and made her grasp it as it throbbed and beat with the excitement under which I was labouring. Her eyes were fixed upon the lovely object thus exposed to her gaze, and I could easily see from the flushing of her face and the sparkling of her eyes what a powerful impression I had made upon her.

All she said was, 'Oh, but if John should know of it.'

I immediately replied, 'But why should John know anything about it? You don't suppose I am such a mean wretch as to tell anybody of what we may do, and if you only keep your own secrets no one need ever know anything about it.

'But perhaps,' I continued, 'you think this little gentleman,' and I shoved the furious member backwards and forwards two or three times in her hand as she still continued to grasp it, 'is not so big as John's and won't give you so much pleasure, but only let me try and I shall do all I can to pleasure you.'

'Oh no, it is not that,' said she hastily, squeezing the little object convulsively in her grasp, and as I bent down to kiss her, she whispered, 'I can't resist you any longer, but you

6

must bolt the door, and if anybody comes I can get away through Miss Laura's room. She won't tell anything; I can easily make her keep quiet.'

This speech not a little astonished me, for from what I knew of Laura I thought she was the last person in the world to make a confidante of her waiting-maid. But I was aware that this was not the moment to expect any explanation, so I jumped out of bed, bolted the door, and speedily returned to the charge, when I found that the opposing party had given up all idea of defence and was quite ready to meet my advances. Stretching herself out in the most favourable position, she allowed me again to mount upon her and, taking hold of the instrument of love, she herself guided it to the proper quarter.

To my surprise, however, the entrance was much more difficult than I had expected and I soon found that I had overrated Master John's capacities and that the fortress, though not a maiden one, had not previously been entered by so large a besieging force. With some little exertion on my part, aided by every means in her power, though she winced a good deal at the pain I put her to, I at length succeeded in effecting my object and penetrated to a depth which from her exclamation of delight when she found me fairly imbedded within her, and from certain other symptoms, I felt certain had never been reached previously. Once fairly established within my new quarter we mutually exerted our utmost endeavours to gratify each other as well as ourselves, and the result of our efforts soon led, much to the satisfaction of both parties, in the temporary subjugation of both the contending forces. Gratified by finding that the issue had been much more satisfactory than I had expected, and not having had an opportunity for some time previously of indulging myself so agreeably, I, much to her surprise and joy, retained possession of the stronghold with my forces so slightly weakened by their late defeat as to give immediate promise of a renewed attack.

7

Telling her to be still for a few minutes and that we should shortly enjoy ourselves again, I began to question her regarding the matters in which I felt interested. I thought it better at first not to allude to Laura, so I commenced by inquiring about John, and I soon found that the one subject led to the other. It appeared that John was the under-groom whose duty it was to attend upon Miss Laura when she rode out. John had courted Betsy for some time previously and had been admitted to all the privileges of a husband on condition that he should marry her as soon as he could obtain a situation which would enable him to support her.

Betsy, it seems, was rather jealous, and John, to tease her, had pretended that he was on terms of intimacy with his young Mistress, a statement for which there was not the slightest foundation. Betsy's suspicions, however, being once roused, were not easily set at rest, and this led her to pay more attention than previously to her young Mistress's proceedings. She had sometimes wondered what induced Laura to go out by herself almost every morning before breakfast, and now fancying that it might be for the purpose of meeting John, she resolved to watch her and ascertain if her suspicions were correct. She accordingly followed her, and found that she invariably made her way to a smaller summer house at a little distance from the house. Here John never made his appearance, but curious to know what Laura was about, Betsy continued her spying until she one day ascertained that, instead of amusing herself with John's article, Miss Laura resorted to the place for the purpose of consoling herself with a very insufficient substitute for what Betsy had suspected to be the offending member.

As Laura slept in the same room with her aunt she had no opportunity of thus indulging herself.

I drew all this gradually from her, leading her on by degrees, and trying to make it appear that I had no particular interest in the subject. Her story, however, had such an effect upon a certain part of my body, which was still imbedded

8

within her, that she could not help feeling as she proceeded with her tale the impression it made upon me. Indeed when she came to relate the discovery she had made, I was obliged to stop her and proceed to a repetition of our enjoyment in order to allay the fire which had been so fiercely lighted up within me. When I had brought the second engagement to a still more satisfactory conclusion than the first, I found it was time for me to get on with my dressing so as not to be too late for dinner, and Betsy volunteered her services to assist as valet. The lewd little monkey, however, was too intent upon examining the course from which she had derived so much pleasure to do anything except fondle and caress it, and seeing the pleasure it evidently gave her, I allowed her to do as she liked. While she amused herself with tickling and squeezing the accessories, handling the principal object, kissing it, inserting it in her mouth and sucking it, and doing everything in her power to restore it to the imposing attitude which had pleased her so much, I endeavoured with as much apparent unconcern as I could assume to ascertain every particular as to Laura.

Betsy however was too quick not to discover what I was after, and said to me, 'Come, come, I see quite well how it is with you – you would like this pretty little gentleman I am playing with to take the place of its substitute between Miss Laura's thighs. Oh! you need not try to deceive me – I felt how it swelled up within me whenever I mentioned her name, and how firm and stiff it grew when I told you what I had seen. Well, it would be almost a pity not to let you take compassion upon her; it is very hard she should be reduced to such a miserable contrivance when she might have such a delicious charmer as this to amuse herself with. But I am afraid you would have some difficulty in getting it in, more than you had with me, why her little plaything is not much bigger than my finger; even John's, though it is not near so big as this, is better than it. But as for this wicked fellow I can hardly grasp it in my hand, and I don't see how you will ever

9

be able to make it enter into such a little chink as she has. However, I dare say you will be able to manage it somehow. Come, I shall make a bargain with you: if you will take John as your groom, so as to let us be married before my belly gets big, as I am afraid it will do after this naughty fellow has been into it, I shall do all I can to enable you to enjoy Miss Laura, and I have no doubt we shall soon find means to accomplish it. What do you say?'

I replied that I was afraid such an arrangement would hardly answer. In the first place, I could not turn away my present servant, and secondly, I was afraid that if John were in my service he might perhaps be apt to be jealous of his master.

She laughed and said that would never do. She, however, soon came to an agreement that I should exert myself to find a better situation for John, and I promised her that if I succeeded with Laura, she should make her a present of fifty pounds as a wedding gift on condition that she acted in all respects as I desired and exerted herself to promote my object and conceal our proceedings from everyone. She stipulated that she was sometimes to have the enjoyment of the charming article which she still continued to fondle, and this I willingly promised, but I warned her that she must be very careful that her Mistress should not suspect our intercourse in the least, as I was quite sure from what I knew of her proud disposition it would ruin all my hopes, as she would never consent to be the rival of her waiting-maid. I easily satisfied her that even for her own sake the utmost caution was absolutely necessary, and having now obtained all the information she could give me and the dinner bell ringing, I hastened to the drawing room.

If I had perceived an alteration in Laura's appearance, she had evidently been no less struck with the change that had taken place in my person, and she expressed her surprise at my having grown so much. I fancied I could perceive that there was some curiosity to ascertain what was the extent of

10

the change which had taken place in a certain quarter, and I caught her eyes more than once glancing in a direction where she must have perceived symptoms of a growth at least corresponding to that of the other parts of my body. I was induced to think that she was by no means displeased with the discovery from her manner towards me, which instead of being as formerly haughty and condescending was now frank and friendly. On entering the drawing room I found that Sir Hugh had not yet made his appearance, and that it would still be a few minutes before we went to dinner. I was conscious that the fingering which Betsy had kept up during the whole time I was dressing had again raised a flame in me which I had not had time to quench, and I turned into the music room to take advantage of the few minutes to calm myself down, that I might not make an exhibition before the rest of the party. Laura had observed me, and thinking that the movement arose from shyness at meeting a party of comparative strangers, she came to me and entered into conversation. The charms of her person, more especially after all that had just passed with Betsy regarding her, again raised the flame to an even greater height than before, and the effect was plainly visible through a pair of thin trousers. I soon saw by her heightened colour that the consequences were not unobserved by her. I was afraid at first that she might be annoyed by so open a demonstration of the effects of her charms, but to my great delight she showed no symptom of being offended, but continued to converse with me, and, I thought, rather enjoyed the confusion which the rampantness of the offending member at first occasioned me. Finding this to be the case, I soon recovered my self-possession, and being desirous to make as great an impression on her senses as possible, I placed myself so that I could not be observed by any of the party in the drawing room, and instead of attempting to conceal it, I allowed the protuberance in front to become even more prominent, indeed so much so, as to enable her to form a pretty accurate idea of its size and shape.

She took no notice of this, but I knew it could not escape her observation. When a general move was made to the dining room, she took my arm and said that, as I was a stranger, I must allow her to take charge of me, until I became a little better acquainted with the company. I willingly assented, and for the rest of the evening I attached myself to her. Without attempting to take any liberties with her, I omitted no opportunity of letting her see the full effect of her beauty and charms upon my senses.

The next morning I was up early and on the lookout. From Betsy's description I had not been able exactly to understand how I could manage to surprise Laura during her amusement, and I determined to watch and follow her and be guided by circumstances. Sometime before the breakfast hour I saw her leave the house by a side door and proceed through a part of the park which was a good deal shaded with trees. I took advantage of the shelter thus afforded me to trace her steps, unperceived, until I came in sight of the summer house, but to my dismay, I found that it was impossible to follow her any further without being discovered. The building was circular, consisting of woodwork to the height of about four feet and above that glass all round. It was situated in the centre of a flower plot of considerable extent in which the bushes were kept down and not allowed to attain any size.

It was therefore admirably adapted for the purpose to which it had been applied, as no one approaching it could well see what passed within, while the party in the interior could command an uninterrupted view all round and discover any intruder at some distance. I was quite aware that it was most important to avoid giving her any alarm or making her suspect I had any idea of her proceedings, and I resolved not to attempt to approach her that morning. So, selecting a tree which was situated in such a manner as to command a complete view of the summer house, I swung myself up into it and soon gained a position from which, with the assistance of a small telescope I had taken with me, I could obtain a good view of her proceedings. I very soon discovered that Betsy's story was perfectly correct. She had apparently no time to spare, for, taking out the little instrument from its place of concealment, she seated herself on a couch from which she could command a view of the approach from the house. Then, extending her thighs, she drew up her petticoats and, inserting the counterfeit article in the appropriate place, began her career of mock pleasure.

I watched all her proceedings with the greatest enjoyment, and such was the effect produced upon me that I could not help following her example. I drew forth my excited member and, as she thrust the little bijou in and out of the delicious cavity in which I so longed to replace it with a better substitute, I responded to every movement of her hand by an up-and-down friction upon the ivory pillar, with such effect that, when she sunk back upon the couch after having procured for herself as much pleasure as such a makeshift could afford, I felt the corresponding efforts produce a similar effect upon my own excited reality, which, throbbing and beating furiously, sent forth a delicious shower of liquid bliss.

I allowed her to get up and return to the house without her perceiving me, and when we met at breakfast she was not even aware I had been out. The day passed very pleasantly. She was evidently flattered with the devotion I showed her and seemed noways indisposed to try to what length her encouragement might carry me, probably thinking that she could at any time check my advances should they become too forward.

In the course of the day I again visited the summer house and ascertained that I had no chance of surprising her there without making some alteration in it, which it would take a little time to effect, but which I resolved to have made if I found I could not succeed otherwise. In the meantime, I resolved to try the effect of a bold stroke.

Getting up early the next morning I proceeded directly to the summer house and waited there till she made her appearance. Having made certain that she was alone, I stretched myself on the couch as nearly as possible in the attitude she had assumed the previous morning. I then unbuttoned my trousers and drew them down below my knees and at the same time turned up my shirt above my waist thus exhibiting the whole forepart of my person entirely naked. Then grasping my stiffly erected weapon in my hand, I exhibited myself performing the same operation which I had witnessed her engaged in the previous morning. She came in without the least suspicion and, on entering the place, had at once a full view of my nearly naked figure extended at full length on the couch and engaged in performing an operation the nature of which she could not possibly misunderstand.

She seemed struck with astonishment – so much that she remained motionless for more than a minute, during which I watched her with intense curiosity. Her face and neck, so far as visible, flushed till they were almost of a purple hue, and her eyes were fixed upon the stiffly erected column up and down which my hand was gently moving. I was in great hopes that the sight had produced the effect I desired. But no. Suddenly recovering herself, she exclaimed, 'For shame, Sir,' and turning away hastily left the place before I had time to rise and interrupt her. I would fain have followed her and tried to induce her to return, but I would not allow my passions to carry me so far as to do what might injure her irreparably in the event of anyone being about the grounds and seeing me in the condition in which I then was.

Before I could replace my dress so as to be able to venture out, she had gone so far that she had reached the house ere I could make up to her.

When we met at breakfast she took no notice of what had passed; nor could I discover any difference in her manner to me, beyond her heightened colour, when we exchanged the morning greeting as if we had not met before. But she carefully avoided any opportunity of our being left alone, though I could sometimes detect her eyes glancing towards me when she thought she was not observed, and more particularly in the direction of the part of which she had obtained a first glance that morning.

Having gone so far with her, I was determined to try at least whether I could not get a little farther. So in the evening when a dance was got up I asked her to waltz with me in such an open manner that she could not easily make any excuse for not doing so. As soon as I got an opportunity of saying a few words unheard, I whispered to her, 'Come, come, Laura, this is too bad of you to be offended at me for doing the very same thing I saw you doing in the same place yesterday morning.'

In an instant her face turned perfectly scarlet and then as pale as death, and I am certain she would have fallen to the ground had I not supported her. In a few seconds she recovered herself a little and in a suppressed but earnest tone she whispered, 'Hush, hush for God's sake.'

I led her out of the room into the conservatory and pressed her to sit down on a bench. She objected to this, saying, 'Not here; not here,' pointing at the same time to the door at the opposite side leading into a rosary which was not overlooked from the drawing room. I there placed her on a seat and sat down beside her and waited for a few minutes, till her emotion should subside.

Finding that she was still quite overcome and remained silent, trembling, and evidently greatly agitated by the discovery that her secret was known to me, I said to her, 'Laura, dearest, you need not be in the least alarmed, your secret is quite safe with me, and nothing shall ever induce me to say a word to anyone regarding it, nor need you fear, my own darling, that I shall take advantage of it to make you do anything you don't like.'

She made no reply but at the same time she offered no

resistance to the caresses I ventured to bestow upon her, and I even fancied that the warm kiss I imprinted on her lips was faintly returned. I went on to say, 'I cannot tell you what bliss it would give me if you would only allow this little charmer to take his proper place, instead of the wretched substitute I so much envied yesterday. I am quite sure it would give you as much pleasure as it would me.' And at the same time, while I supported her with one arm round her waist, I placed her hand upon the object to which I drew her attention, and which, throbbing fiercely, lay extended along my thigh. Emboldened by her allowing her hand to remain upon it, I unbuttoned a few buttons and removed my shirt, when out it started stiff and erect as a piece of ivory. When I again placed her hand upon it, I felt it grasped with convulsive eagerness. Excited beyond measure by this, I slipped my hand under her dress, bringing it up along her thighs until it reached the object of my adoration, and gently insinuated a finger within its moist lips.

The touch of my finger, however, within such a sensitive spot seemed to rouse her at once, for she started up, saying, 'Not now, Frank, not now, dearest. You must let me go. I must have time to think over this. I know you won't refuse me when I tell you I cannot remain with you at present. There, that is a good boy, go back to the drawing room, and I shall follow you immediately.' At the same time she gave a fond pressure on the sensitive plant she still held in her grasp, imprinted a warm kiss on my lips, and then tore herself from my arms.

I felt that the place was not such as to enable me to attempt to carry the matter farther at present, and delaying for a minute or two in the conservatory that I might calm down my excitement a little, I slipped quietly back to the drawing room. To cover the agitation I still felt, I again joined in the waltz with the first partner I could find. In a few minutes Laura returned to the room, nor could anyone have possibly discovered from her manner that she had so recently undergone such violent emotion. I could hardly believe it possible that the seemingly proud and haughty girl was the same panting, trembling creature who had so recently been in my arms.

I soon, however, found reason to regret I had not chosen a more fitting reason for my denouement, in which case I might perhaps have turned it to greater profit than I appeared likely to do. With the morning, she had recovered all her coolness and self-possession, and had evidently determined on the course she was to pursue. She did not leave her room till breakfast time, and afterwards evaded all my stratagems to obtain a private interview with her.

After luncheon the horses were brought to the door, and a large party started out for a ride. When we had gone a short distance, she contrived to let the others get ahead of us, so as to leave us alone together, for I had got her to dispense with Master John's attendance when I accompanied her. She then turned up a quiet lane which led to a common where there was little chance of our meeting anyone, and where the many bushes, scattered in large clumps over it, were high enough to conceal us from observation.

Then, without any hesitation, she entered at once on the subject which engrossed all my thoughts. She said she could not imagine how I could possibly have discovered her secret, but that as it was clear I had done so, it was no use for her now to attempt to deny it, and that she was quite sure I would not make any use of it that could be injurious to her.

'But don't suppose,' said she, 'that I am offended at the manner you took of showing me you had found out my propensity. It was a very good idea, and I shall be delighted to become better acquainted with my new friend,' at the same time placing her hand upon him. 'He is a very handsome little fellow, but I must tell you frankly that though I shall be happy to contribute as far as I safely can to afford him amusement, you must not expect that I can allow him to do what might get me into most serious difficulties. Perhaps

17

after a time even this may be managed, but at present it is out of the question, so he must be contented for the present with the pleasures I can safely afford him.'

As she spoke, she continued to unbutton my trousers and remove my shirt, until she had fairly uncovered her new acquaintance, which started out under the pressure of her soft fingers showing his head proudly erect. She loaded it with caresses, at the same time expressing in the warmest terms her admiration of its size and beauty. I saw at once from her manner that she had made her mind up on the subject and that there was no chance of complete success on that occasion at least. So I resolved to make the best of the opportunity and humour her inclination, and do all in my power to gratify her in her own way, trusting that on some more propitious occasion I might obtain my wishes in their fullest extent.

Ascertaining, therefore, that there was no one in sight and that we were in such a position as to be able to command a view all round of some considerable distance so that no one could approach us without being observed, I said that all I desired was to contribute to her happiness, and that I only wanted to know in what manner that could be best done, and that I was quite ready to use every exertion in my power to effect it; that if she had any curiosity about her new acquaintance, I was quite prepared to do anything I could to gratify her. She said she was curious about it, and would be delighted to have a better view of it and see what it could do.

I immediately unbuttoned my braces and let down my trousers and tucked up my shirt under my waistcoat, then, bringing my leg over the horse so as to sit on one side in her own fashion, exposed everything to her view. She seemed perfectly enchanted as she took hold of and played with the ivory column and uncovered its ruby head and explored the secrets of the pendant receptacles of the liquid of life. She seemed to be fully aware of the effect of her soft hand moving up and down upon the object of her worship, and she watched with eagerness the consequences her operation produced. I did not attempt to conceal my emotions from her in the least, and gave myself up to the voluptuous sensations which her proceedings could not fail to occasion, till they attained such a height that a full overflow of the precious liquid, spouting from the overexcited tube, fairly attested the effect produced upon me. She gazed upon the charming sight with evident delight, and dwelt upon every excited motion I made, endeavouring by every means in her power to heighten and increase my enjoyment.

When I had in some measure recovered from the pleasure-trance, I threw my arms around her and thanked her for all the pleasure she had afforded me and said it was not fair that I should enjoy all the delight, and I trusted she would allow me to repeat upon her the lesson she had thus practised on me. She said at once that she would not get off the horse, but that if it would afford me any pleasure she was quite willing that I should do anything I liked with her in that position. I saw it was no use to attempt more, so I resolved to make the most of my situation.

Dismounting from my horse, I removed her leg from the horn of the saddle, and raising up her clothes discovered her most exquisite thighs and the enchanting object between them almost completely hidden under a cluster of dark-auburn curly hair. After kissing and caressing it for some minutes, parting the moist lips, and tickling the surrounding moss, I tried to introduce my finger. The tightness of the aperture and the difficulty I had in getting it in beyond an inch or two soon satisfied me that either the pain or the fear of doing mischief had prevented her from using the substitute to such an extent as to deprive the first living entrant of the glory and pleasure of a victory over her virgin charms, and this discovery increased tenfold the desire I felt to be the conqueror in such a splendid field of battle. I did the best I could in the situation in which I was placed, and partly with my finger and partly with my tongue I succeeded in creating such a degree of titillation upon her sensitive clitoris and the adjacent parts that, sided as it was by the excitement of the scene that had previously been enacted, it produced such an effect upon her as she had never previously experienced. When her convulsive motions ceased, and the stream flowed over my fingers down her thighs, she bent down her head and fondly kissed me, acknowledging that I had contrived to afford her more pleasure than she had believed it possible she could enjoy.

I seized the opportunity to point out to her the effect which her wanton hand had upon my champion, for she had now bent down to grasp it and play with it again and it still held up its proud head as erect as ever. I endeavoured to persuade her that what she had experienced was nothing in comparison with the bliss he could bestow upon her. But she remained firm, and would not allow me to give her a practical illustration of my theory, though she was so delighted with her little friend that she continued to caress and fondle him whenever she could, almost all the way till we reached home.

Two or three scenes of this nature followed in the course of the few following days, and still I could not contrive to get further with her. I therefore resolved to try the effect of a stratagem that had occurred to me. Though she had resisted all my entreaties to meet me at the summer house, I had told her the day after our explanation that I would not act so cruelly to her as she did to me, and that I was desirous to contribute to her amusement in any manner she liked best, and, therefore, as she seemed determined that her visits to the summer house should be solitary ones, I would put some books and pictures in the hiding-place which I was sure would divert her and add to her enjoyment whenever she would take a fancy to repair thither. I kept a watch upon her, but never could catch her there, though I soon became aware from the change in position of the books that she occasionally visited the place when she knew I was away and could not surprise her.

I selected a day on which a party was made up to visit some

objects of curiosity in the neighbourhood, and when she had announced her intention to stay at home, having already been often at the place, and to allow another lady of the party to ride her horse. In the morning I arranged with my groom that he should file off the heads of the nails of one of my horse's shoes, so that the shoe should come off easily, and I appointed him to meet me a short distance from the house on the road we were to take.

After I had proceeded with the party for a few miles, I pretended to think that my horse was going lame, and dismounting, I exhibited one foot with the shoe nearly off. As the horse was a valuable one, the excuse was readily accepted that I could not proceed farther, but must walk him back quietly. As soon, however, as the party had got out of sight, by the aid of a hammer and a few nails I had taken in my pocket, I fastened the shoe, and started back at full speed. Meeting my groom at the place I had appointed, I told him to get the horse properly shod and then take him to a small inn in a retired place a few miles off, so as not to have my return known at the hall. I then hastened to make my way across the fields to the summer house, having a strong hope that Laura would take advantage of the opportunity for visiting it, as my absence would render it safe for her to do so and would at the same time preclude the chance of her being able to have any gratification in my company and reduce her to her solitary amusement.

On making a more minute inspection of the summer house, I had discovered a circumstance which was not apparent at first sight and which had inspired me with the idea of my present operation. The ceiling was formed of small branches, split and nailed together in the form of panels. One of these, I discovered, was moveable and gave access to a small apartment above, part of which was floored over and occasionally used by the gardener to dry seeds. To this apartment the only access was by means of a ladder. The ceiling however was low enough to admit of my catching hold of the sides of the opening when standing on a stool, and thus swinging myself up into the interior. I had contrived, by means of oiling the hinges well and attaching a weight with a pulley, to make the entrance open easily and without the least noise, and I had also made some small apertures in the roof from which I could keep a lookout.

I immediately took possession of my hiding place and closed the entrance, resolved to take the chance of Laura's coming if I had to wait there the whole day, for I knew the precaution I had taken would prevent anything being known of my being in the neighbourhood until the return of the party, who had made the necessary arrangements for taking refreshments with them, and were not to be back till the evening.

I waited with patience all the forenoon, comforted with the idea that in all probability Laura would find herself at leisure after luncheon, at which time some of the elder part of the company who had not joined the expedition usually drove out.

It happened as I had anticipated and very soon after the ordinary luncheon hour I was rejoiced to see Laura approaching. I was very certain, from the manner in which she looked about her as she drew near, what her object was, and I made my arrangements before she arrived so as to be able to keep perfectly still till the proper time came. After taking a walk round the place apparently to make certain that no one was in the neighbourhood, she came in, and taking out one of the books, sat down to peruse it. Convinced that my only chance of success was to catch her in the critical moment when she would be too much overwhelmed by her voluptuous sensations to offer any resistance, and afraid that any precipitate movement on my part might enable her to retain that self-command of which she possessed so large a share, I waited quietly for the effect of the seductive entertainment I had provided for her. Nor was it long before it began to produce the expected result. Her colour heightened, she moved backwards and forwards upon the couch apparently unconsciously, and at last her fingers stole under her petticoats and reached the part which was the principal scene of her excitement and which I could see from the motions of her arm she was attempting to allay. In a few minutes she appeared to be unable longer to withstand the temptation which the opportunity offered, and rising up, she went to the hiding-place and took from it some lascivious pictures and the little object with which she intended to solace herself.

After heightening her desires by an attentive examination of the seductive plates, she raised her dress and stretched herself on the couch, much in the same attitude in which I had previously seen her, and after a little toying with her finger she separated the ruby lips and introduced the mock representation of that part of me which I was so eager to enable her to judge how much more pleasure the reality would afford her. Even then I had the patience to wait until she had made use of it for some little time and until I could discern from sundry sighs that the pleasure it was giving her was approaching a climax. Then gently raising the trap door and catching hold of the sides, I quietly let myself drop into the apartment below. A slight rustling noise I made attracted her attention, and looking up from her book, she beheld my almost naked body with the most prominent object of it standing fiercely erect, for I had let down my trousers and turned up my shirt so as to afford her a complete view of my person.

At this sight, so suddenly and unexpectedly presented to her, without her at first being able to discover who it was that thus presented himself in such a guise, she was so struck with surprise and astonishment that she was in the utmost consternation and completely lost her presence of mind, remaining motionless even after I had fully appeared before her and approached her so that she must have recognised me. Aware that, if I was to profit by the opportunity, I must not lose a moment in explanation, I at once got between her thighs which were stretched out widely extended, and withdrawing the wretched mock article from its darling retreat, I threw myself upon her and instantly without the least hesitation replaced it with reality. I was quite aware I should find some difficulty in getting admission, but most fortunately her situation was so extremely favourable that I was enabled so far to effect my object as to get the head of my weapon fairly inserted within the delicious lips of her charmer before she had recovered from her surprise sufficiently to offer any opposition. Then, indeed, she attempted to rise up, exclaiming, 'Oh! Frank, Frank, this will never do.' By this time, however, I had got my arms fairly round her waist and held her locked in a close embrace, and while I endeavoured to stifle her remonstrances with burning kisses on her fair lips, I exerted my utmost efforts to improve my position. My thrusts and heaves, driven with the greatest vigour my burning passion could inspire me with, evidently hurt her severely, but this I had expected and was fully prepared for, as I was aware from my previous inspections of the charming spot that it never had been stretched to such an extent as to enable me to attain free admission, and consequently I was not disposed to relax in my efforts on that account, trusting that the overwhelming pleasure that would ensue would fully make up for all suffering, and that I should obtain full possession, as soon as she should be enabled to join in my transports.

Her very struggles, caused partly by pain and partly by apprehension, as she endeavoured to rise up, only aided me in effecting my purpose, and after a short contest, I had the satisfaction and delight of feeling the resistance which her virgin obstacles had offered to my progress entirely give way, and my victorious champion had penetrated her inmost secret recesses in such an effectual manner as to produce the most delicious conjunction of the most sensitive parts of our bodies that can possibly be conceived. The effect upon her, however, was not so immediately delightful as it was upon me. The pain occasioned by the last few thrusts by which I had completed the achievement had been so severe as to make her abandon her resistance, and when it suddenly ceased, on my weapon obtaining complete entrance, she sank back on the couch as if exhausted. I followed her example and sank down upon her, pressing her more closely in my arms, and being now relieved from the necessity of using force, I regulated the movements of my victorious champion so as to try to avoid as far as possible giving her any further pain, and endeavoured to replace it with more delightful sensations. But with the removal of the pain her apprehensions revived, and she again entreated me to let her rise. Her request, however, now came too late – even had I been disposed to comply with it, which I certainly was not, the excited state into which she had worked herself previous to my appearing on the scene had produced such an effect upon her frame that very few up-and-down movements of my pleasure-giver within the now thoroughly opened up premises were quite sufficient to remove all traces of the pain and to produce the consummation he was labouring to effect and was so eager to join in. Before she had time to repeat her request and even before I was quite prepared to respond to the tide of joy, her head again sank back and she exclaimed, 'Oh! Oh! Delicious, oh! Dearest, oh! I can bear it no longer.' Her extatic movements, while in the act of enjoyment, were all that was required to make me join in her delight, and pouring forth a torrent of bliss I sank motionless on her breast enjoying a happiness that may be conceived but cannot possibly be described.

When I had recovered a little from my transports, still retaining my place, I thought it was time to endeavour to appease her indignation which I feared might have been aroused at the trap I had evidently laid for her. But I soon found I had no occasion to be alarmed on this subject. She had no hesitation in admitting that, though she had so long resisted my entrance, it had only been from the fear of the consequences and she had all along been as anxious as I was for the crowning pleasure from the first moment when she had viewed the potent charms of my pleasure-giver, and she had been as much disappointed and annoyed at the unsatisfactory manner in which our intercourse had hitherto been conducted; and she even went on to say that whatever the consequences might be to her she was rejoiced I had had the courage to make her break through the restraint she had imposed on herself.

Accordingly, when I asked her whether her new acquaintance had not justified, by the result he had produced, all that I had predicted as the consequences of his being admitted into his present delicious quarter, she frankly confessed that though she at first had suffered dreadfully from the tearing open of her interior, the final close had much more than gratified all her expectation and had fully made up for all she had endured. And she added that she never would have forgiven me, if I had yielded to her entreaties and left the performance unfinished.

'But now,' said she, 'that this little darling has done his duty so well, do get up and take a look about, in case anyone should stray in this direction. I don't want to part with you so soon, but it would never do for anyone to come in and catch us in this situation.'

'No, no, dearest,' I replied, 'you only half enjoyed yourself the last time, and I am afraid if I were to withdraw this little gentleman I might have to give you more pain in replacing him, and as I want you thoroughly to enter into all the blissful sensations of this occasion, you must let him remain where he is.'

'What,' said she, 'do you mean to say he can do it again? Oh! That would be delicious! But I am so frightened for anyone coming.'

'Well, dearest, just keep your arms round me, and I shall raise you up till we can take a look about us.' And clasping her round the waist so as to keep us still firmly united by the pleasantest of all links, I raised her up to a position from which we could command a view all round us, and thus satisfy ourselves that all was safe.

Then gently laying her down, I again commenced operations; at first thrusting my weapon cautiously and gradually in and out of the charming orifice so as to avoid the risk of hurting her. But I soon found there was no danger of this. The elements of pleasure were so fiercely aroused within her that my exertions occasioned very different sensations from those which had accompanied my first entrance into her delicious quarters, and in a few minutes her efforts to promote our mutual bliss vied with, if they did not exceed, my own. For the first time in her life she thoroughly enjoyed the most exquisite of all sensations a woman can be blessed with, that of having her most sensitive region fully gorged with the masterpiece which first works her up to the most amorous frenzy and then subdues her by making her die away with itself in melting bliss. There was not a moment from the time when I half withdrew and again inserted the delicious morsel, the possession of which she so much enjoyed, till the overwhelming bliss of mutual emission took away our senses, that she did not evince both by her gestures and her words the most excessive and frantic delight, and I need hardly say that my enjoyment equalled hers.

When our second course was finished, I withdrew my still unexhausted weapon, which notwithstanding its double victory still held up its head bravely, but I was somewhat horrified at the mingled tide which now poured out its crimson stream down her thighs. She was in great distress less it might betray her, but I managed to prevent any of it getting upon her dress and persuaded her to accompany me to a small fountain a little way off where, dipping my handkerchief in the water, I first removed all marks of the conflict, and then continued to bathe the swollen and tender lips which still bore traces of the fierce nature of the combat. Finding the cooling sensation was grateful to her, I continued the application until the sight of her charms, thus freely exposed, made the author of the mischief so wild at the contemplation of the effects of his own deeds that I was obliged to show the state he was in, and tell her that it would require another defeat before he could be quited. She hesitated a little from the fear of the pain accompanying his re-entrance in the present tender state of her interior. But seeing that he also bore bloody marks of the fray, she insisted on reciprocating the good offices I had bestowed upon her, and taking the handkerchief, she proceeded to remove them by tenderly bathing the little gentleman.

Pretty well aware what would be the consequence of this proceeding, I allowed her to take her own way. And as even the application of the cold water failed to quench his ardour, she at length admitted that there was nothing for it but to renew the combat and we accordingly returned to the summer house.

Notwithstanding all my care, the pain I occasioned her while getting fairly established within her was very severe; but she persevered in her efforts to introduce him to his old quarters until she had effectually accomplished it to our mutual satisfaction. As soon as I had fairly reached the bottom, I desisted from the attack, and allowed her to remain quiet till all her suffering had entirely subsided and she was again in a condition to be able to enjoy the perfect pleasure.

The first hot eagerness of novelty being now over, we both felt disposed on this occasion to prolong our enjoyment as much as possible and we accordingly proceeded with the operation more leisurely, watching the effects to our mutual efforts to produce the greatest enjoyment, and telling each other when to quicken or retard our movements, so as to keep the delicious sensations at their highest pitch, and at the same time delay the final crisis as long as possible. Sometimes it was I who would urge the fierce intruder backwards and forwards in his career of pleasure; and sometimes, making me remain still, it was she who, with up-and-down heaves of her delicious buttocks, would make the lips and sides of her charming, tight-fitting sheath move over my entranced weapon, creating within it the most voluptuous sensations it is possible to conceive. But at length we could restrain ourselves no longer, and then again commenced a furious struggle of mutual heaves and thrusts intermingled with burning kisses and fond caresses, which soon resulted in drawing from us a pleasing stream of such enchanting extasy that Laura declared it was even more delicious than the previous one, which she had believed could not have been surpassed.

By this time she began to be afraid that her absence might be noticed and insisted that it was time for her to return to the hall. Before she left me I easily persuaded her to resume her morning visits to the summer house, and to allow me to meet her there. I satisfied her that there was no risk in this, as in the event of anyone coming to the place by chance, I could easily take refuge in my hiding-place so that no suspicion could arise if she were found there alone.

For several mornings we continued to indulge ourselves with a repetition of our amorous pranks and every meeting only added to the zest with which we gave ourselves up to every mode of enjoyment we could devise.

The sole drawback to our pleasures was the impossibility in such an exposed situation of enjoying the sight and the touch at once of the whole of each other's charms, and I anxiously watched for any opportunity when we might be able to accomplish this. One forenoon Lady Middleton had accompanied the rest of the party on a visit to some friends in the neighbourhood from which they were not to return till night, leaving at home only Sir Hugh, Miss Middleton, Laura, and myself. I had made some excuse for not accompanying the party, but my real reason was the wish to have an opportunity of meeting Laura, as she had been unable to keep her appointment with me that morning, though I little expected that I was to be thereby enabled to arrange for the full accomplishment of our most anxious wishes.

I was sitting with the two ladies when a servant brought in a note for Miss Middleton saying that the messenger waited for an answer. She read it and said to Laura, 'This is very provoking, it is a note from Mr Percival asking me to come over and meet the Savilles at dinner. I should like so much to go, as all our party are away to-day, and I shall not have another opportunity of meeting my old friends; but I am afraid there is no conveyance to take me. If the pony were able to go, I should drive over in the pony-chaise, but I fear he is not sufficiently recovered from his accident.'

Laura's eyes and mine met, and all the advantage of getting her aunt away for the night flashed upon us. I gave her a look to urge her aunt to go. She reflected for a minute, and then said she did not think the pony was fit for work yet, but that her aunt might send for a carriage from the town, which was some miles distant, and that she would arrange with her mother to come for her the next morning.

To this, however, Miss Middleton objected, saying that before a messenger could go on foot and bring the carriage it would be too late, even if he succeeded in getting it, which was doubtful.

I now thought I might venture to interfere, and addressing Miss Middleton I said, 'I did not think you would have treated me with so much ceremony. You know there are two horses of mine standing idle in the stable which are quite at your service; if you wish to send a messenger into town, my servant shall go directly, but I think the best plan will be for you to allow me to drive you over in my dogcart, and as you may not like coming home in the dark, I shall come back for you tomorrow at any hour you may fix.' She appeared to hesitate, but Laura had little difficulty in persuading her to accept my offer. She accordingly went to prepare, while I ordered the dogcart to be got ready. Before setting out I arranged with Laura that as it might appear strange were I to insist on returning to dinner when she was alone at home with her father, I should, if invited, remain at the Percivals till evening. She agreed to go to bed at her usual hour and to leave the door connecting her room and mine unlocked and to tie a white ribbon to the door-handle, if all was safe for me to come to her. I started with Miss Middleton, and as I had expected was urged to remain till next day. I at once agreed to stay for dinner, but refused all their pressing to remain all night on the plea that I had made no preparations for so doing. I remained till pretty late and then started for the Hall, promising to return the next forenoon for Miss Middleton.

By the time I arrived everyone had gone to bed, and I hastened to follow their example.

My first impulse was to examine Laura's door, and I was rejoiced to find the agreed-on signal. I hastily stripped off my clothes, and opening the door softly, found her still awake, awaiting my arrival. Throwing down the bed clothes I was about to jump into her arms, when it occurred to me that the operations we contemplated might perhaps leave some traces behind, which might lead to suspicion if discovered in her bed. I therefore said to her that it would be safer for her to repair with me to mine. Ascertaining that her door was locked so as to prevent all intrusion, I took her round the waist and led her to my room.

As soon as we reached the bedside I threw off my shirt and said, 'Now, dearest, since we have at last obtained the long desired opportunity we must endeavour to avail ourselves of it to the best of our abilities. I shall try to contribute as much as I can to your happiness and I am sure you will not hesitate to do anything in your power to add to mine. Now, the first thing to be done is to get rid of all these obstacles to my fully seeing and enjoying all your charms.'

She made no objection to my removing the envious veil which covered her person. Indeed I think she was quite as anxious as I was to enjoy the delight which the contemplation of each other's beauties was sure to produce upon us.

31

However, at last we were both too eager to enjoy the *summum bonum* of earthly felicity to give up much time to the preliminaries.

After a cursory inspection of each other's persons, I stretched her at full length upon the bed and getting upon her I made her herself insert my stiffly distended champion into her delicious pleasure-sheath, and enabled her for the first time to enjoy the delicious sensation occasioned by the complete contact in every quarter of our naked bodies. Making her clasp her arms around me, and twist her thighs and legs about my hips, I drove my rammer into her as far as it would go and then commenced a more voluptuous encounter than any we had yet sustained. Fired by the sight she had enjoyed of my naked person and animated by the delicious sensations which our close contact was sure to occasion, she responded at once to all my movements and there ensued a fierce combat between us, each of us striving by every artifice and exertion in our power to prove the victor, and while conquering, to add to the enjoyment of the vanquished. She proved the conqueror by forcing me to be the first to yield up my tribute; but not wishing to be outdone in the capacity of confering pleasure, I continued my vigorous heaves and thrusts in the delicious receptacle in which I was engulfed, while I felt the warm life-drops bursting from me in a torrent of bliss, until I was sensible that she also had yielded to the potent spell and shared my enjoyment by mingling her contribution with the tide which flowed from me. Then with a warm kiss we ceased our efforts and lay for a while locked in each other's arms, still joined together by the tender tie that bound us in a perfect heaven of luxurious delight.

If we could have reckoned upon a similar enjoyment every night, we would both have remained thus closely embracing for the whole night without desiring greater pleasure.

But the slight view of her splendid charms I had already enjoyed had only heightened my desire for a more minute inspection of them, and I could not afford to lose the opportunity thus fortunately presented to me. Getting up, therefore, and lighting some additional candles I had prepared for the purpose, I stretched her out all naked as she was on the bed and commenced a thorough examination of all those beauties which I had so eagerly longed to inspect, and which as yet I had only been able partially and cursorily to investigate. No part of her escaped my ardent gaze and eager touch. She willingly yielded to my wishes, nay, she even seemed gratified by my eagerness, and placed herself in every position in which she fancied I should be able to detect a new beauty. Every portion of her body, both before and behind, was in succession the object of my adoration and was covered with the most passionate and thrilling kisses and caresses. The effect of this may easily be imagined, and it was not long before the imposing majesty of my overjoyed pleasure-giver showed to her, and equally convinced me, of the necessity we were under of cooling our ardour by a repetition of the same delightful process which we had already undergone.

After this was happily concluded, she insisted on having in her turn the same privilege I had enjoyed, and she made me undergo the same minute investigation to which she had been subjected. Her curiosity was excessive; every object underwent the most searching examination and of course all those parts in which there was a difference between us were more particularly and vigorously explored and discussed. It was impossible for me to remain insensible to her lascivious caresses which again roused the fire within me. My staff of love started up proud and erect as if eager to exhibit its full proportions to her ardent gaze. Upon me the effect was most delicious. To find myself lying there stark naked before a lovely girl and undergoing the delightful touches with which she covered every part of my person as she explored my most secret charms, and at the same time to gaze on all her splendid beauties which were as freely exposed before me, was bliss indeed which roused me to the highest pitch of excitement, and again I repaid her in the most delicious manner for all the pleasing sensations her charming researches had excited in me. After this we lay for some time in each other's arms luxuriating in the blissful feelings caused by our complete conjunction, till morning beginning to appear, I suggested that she should endeavour to obtain a little repose to prevent the fatigues of the night exhibiting their traces upon her too obviously the next day. Not yet satisfied, however, she laid her hand on the weapon of love, as if to ascertain whether it was yet capable of again conferring upon her the bliss she desired. Quite understanding and appreciating her object, I soon satisfied her in the most practical manner that his powers were by no means wholly exhausted, and having achieved another victory over our raging desires, we at length fell asleep locked in each other's arms.

When I awoke, the sun was shining brightly into the room. During her sleep Laura had somewhat changed her position, and instead of fronting me, had turned upon her left side, presenting her splendid posteriors to me, between which my champion was nestling himself. Judging by his imposing appearance, his powers did not seem in any way impaired by the exertions of the previous night. Turning down the bed-clothes, I for some time quietly revelled in the sight of her charms, and then getting excited beyond endurance, though unwilling to disturb her peaceful slumber, I thought I might perhaps be able without awakening her to take up a more satisfactory position than the one I enjoyed. So gently raising her right leg and creeping as close behind her as I could, I placed my right leg between her thighs in such a manner that my champion shoved himself between her legs, stretching up almost to her navel. In this position I lay for some little time till some half muttered words and certain movements of her body made me suspect that Laura in her sleep was acting over again the scenes of the previous night. Convinced that she would have no more objection than

34

myself to the illusion being converted into the reality, I gently separated the lips of the seat of pleasure and inserted the tip of the appropriate organ. His sweet touch in such a sensitive spot at once broke her slumber. She opened her eyes, and glancing downward got a full view of my stiffly distended weapon with its ruby head quite uncovered just entering within the charming precincts of her lovely retreat, and she said smiling that it was just what she had been dreaming of. She was then going to turn herself round towards me, but I told her to remain as she was and that I thought we should be able to accomplish our wishes in that position. I pointed out to her that although we could not so well enjoy the pleasure of kissing each other, we could at least better watch and observe each other's operations while my weapon was perforating her, as the reflexion of our figures in a large mirror, which I had purposely placed so as to produce the best effect, would add greatly to our enjoyment. Looking towards it, she blushed deeply at beholding exposed to her full view her own lovely face, exquisite swelling breasts, snow-white belly and ivory thighs, with the upper part of the mount of pleasure beautifully shaded with its appropriate fringe and the lips swollen and distended with the shaft of love, while my leg, holding her thighs apart, exposed to view between them the pleasure-yielding receptacles of its liquid treasures, and at every heave I gave exhibited at full length the staff of my weapon as I alternately penetrated and then partly withdrew it from its delicious sheath. This exquisite sight delighted us so much that we determined to prolong it as much as possible, and regulating each other's movements so as to keep up the enjoyment to the uttermost and at the same time hold back the crisis, we lay in the most ecstatic bliss for upwards of an hour, enjoying the thrilling delight which this perfect combination of the most exquisite sensations of touch and sight can confer. At length, in spite of our endeavours, we could no longer restrain the tide of passion, a few furious heaves of my maddened and thrusting pleasure-giver completed our bliss, and the genial shower sprinkled the field of pleasure and calmed our overexcited senses.

One other soul-stirring enjoyment was all we had time to accomplish before the approach of the hour at which Laura was usually called warned us that we must separate, and with the most poignant regret that we might not have another opportunity of again enjoying ourselves in such a delightful manner, we parted.

In the forenoon I drove out for Miss Middleton. As her friends wished her to remain, I of course endeavoured to persuade her to do so and offered to come back for her on any day she might fix, but she insisted on returning home that day. I had, however, the satisfaction of finding that she had made an arrangement with the friends whom she had gone to meet to pay them a visit for some weeks as soon as they returned to their own abode, which they were to do in about a week.

One circumstance, however, occurred the same day which rather counterbalanced the pleasure with which I received this intelligence. Young Master Frank on leaving school had gone to pay a visit to a school-fellow, but a letter had arrived from him that morning to say that he would be home the next day. Now his arrival and consequent occupation of the room between Laura's and mine threatened to prevent the constant agreeable intercourse which I had expected to be able to keep up with her during her aunt's absence.

I felt very much annoyed at the idea, and urged her, if possible, to get some arrangement made by which he might occupy some other apartment. She said, however, that she was afraid to make any such proposal to her mother for fear of exciting suspicions as to her object, or of occasioning my removal to another room, which would be equally destructive for our projects.

On the whole she took the matter so quietly and coolly that I was rather astonished, considering the enjoyment she evidently had in our intercourse. A little annoyed at this, I

36

made up my mind that if my young friend retained any portion of the youthful beauty I remembered him to possess, I would endeavour if possible to make up in his arms for the enjoyment he would deprive me of by keeping me out of his sister's.

His first appearance at once decided me to follow out the idea that had occurred to me. At sixteen, some years younger than his sister and just of that delightful age when the passions of manhood have begun to exert their influence on the senses but before thay have taken away the attractive and charming bloom and graces of youth, he was, if possible, more captivating than his sister. Indeed, when upon one occasion I dressed him up as a girl, it was almost impossible to distinguish between them and he might easily have passed for her even among her intimate acquaintances. We became good friends at once. When the ladies left the table after dinner, I made a sign to him to come over beside me, and he was very soon communicating to me all his secrets. I easily led him to talk of his school-fellows and their amusements, and when the party rose to join the ladies he was in the midst of the details of the history of one of the elder boys to whom a married lady had taken a fancy at a house where he had been visiting, and who had conferred a favour on him of which it was very evident my young friend was somewhat envious. When we went to the drawing room, he wanted to continue the history, but I said to him that it would be better not to do so there, but that as he slept in the next room to mine, he might come to me after we had retired for the night, when we would have a better opportunity for discussing the subject. He said he would, but that I was not to expect him till everyone had gone to bed, in case his mother or sister should come into his room. Although a little surprised at this allusion to the latter, I was quite satisfied from what he said that all was right, as, unless he somewhat comprehended my object, he would not have thought it necessary to make any mystery or take any precaution on the subject.

I went to bed, and taking a book, remained awake reading until I heard my door open, and my young friend entered with only his nightshirt on. When he came to the bedside I at once threw down the bed-clothes and made room for him beside me. He jumped in instantly, and clasping him in my arms I pressed him to my bosom. He warmly returned my embrace, and the idea I had formed as to his appreciating my intentions was immediately confirmed by my finding something hard and stiff pressing against my belly, and I soon managed to ascertain that his instrument was in a state of fierce erection. After a few kisses and caresses, I led to the subject of his young friend and the lady, asking how old he was, and then laying my hand upon his organ of pleasure, asked him whether his friend's plaything was bigger than this. He said at once it was, and then taking hold of mine, which as may be supposed was standing stiff enough, he added that it was not so big as mine. Continuing to caress his little charmer, I said I was afraid it was a very naughty little gentleman, and asked whether he had ever had a lady to teach him how to behave himself properly. He said, 'Oh! no! I have not been so fortunate, but I do wish I could get someone to do it with me. I can think of nothing else night or day, and I shall go wild unless I can manage it before long.'

The manner in which my caresses affected him showed plainly how excitable he was. He pressed me to him, and as I grasped his instrument he twisted himself backwards and forwards endeavouring to make my hand serve as a substitute for what he so eagerly desired, while he begged of me to tell him whether I could not put him in the way of obtaining fulfillment of his wishes. I at once promised that if he would get permission to pay me a visit at the Hall, I would arrange that he should have as much of it as he liked, if he would only allow me to witness and participate with him in his pleasures. In his delight and gratitude he at once said that he would do anything I liked, that I had only to tell what I wanted and he would be as eager as I could be to do whatever was in his power that would contribute to my enjoyment.

During this conversation I had been playing with his pretty little instrument as he had been with mine, and I had occasionally introduced it between my thighs squeezing them together so as to compress it between them and meeting and returning the thrusts which he could not help giving on finding his little charmer so agreeably tickled by my soft flesh. This drew from him exclamations of delight.

'Why, my dear boy,' said I, 'if this gives you pleasure, as I imagine it does, I think I could manage to make you do it in a manner that will be more agreeable still.' Turning round to him I presented to him my posteriors, and retaining hold of his instrument I inserted it between my hips, and squeezing and pressing it in the same manner as formerly, I enabled him to enjoy the pleasing friction over a larger portion of the surface of his now inflamed weapon. This seemed to gratify him extremely, and he repeatedly thanked me for the nice way in which he said I made him do it, and protested that he had never enjoyed it so much before. I told him I thought I could make it even pleasanter still. I had still retained my fingers round the root of his sensitive plant, and I now drew it back a little, and raising the point, directed it to the orifice between the cheeks of my posteriors. Opening the lips so as to permit the head to penetrate a short way, I made the cheeks of my bottom close round the head of the intruder so as to produce a most delicious compression upon it, which drew from him the exclamation, 'Oh! This is splendid!'

I then asked him whether he had ever put it in here before. He seemed a little surprised at the question, and said, 'No,' and then putting down his hand and ascertaining the little charmer's head was actually within the lips of the orifice, he immediately asked, 'Will it go in?'

'Just try, my dear boy,' was my answer.

He did not wait for any pressing, but immediately pressed forwards, and as I favoured the insertion as much as I could, a very few thrusts sufficed to lodge the charming intruder fairly within me, evidently as much to his delight as it was to mine. As soon as it was driven completely home, and his thighs and belly came in close contact with my buttocks, he ceased his movements and lay still for some minutes apparently in the greatest ecstasy. The complete constriction which was thus established on every part of his stiff-standing instrument – so tightly fitting and pressing upon it and yet so deliciously tender and soft – was so different from anything he had ever previously felt, when his own or a school-fellow's hand had procured from him an emission, it seemed quite to overpower him.

After fully enjoying himself for a little time, he withdrew the inflamed morsel which I felt burning hot within me, bringing it out nearly to its full extent and then replacing it.

He then said, 'Tell me, my dear fellow, may I do this, it is so delicious, but I am afraid of hurting you.'

'Hurting me?' I replied. 'You need not be very afraid of that. Does that feel as if you were hurting me,' taking his hand and placing it upon my inflamed member of which in his excitement he had lost his hold, and which throbbing and burning stood up fiercely erected along my belly, excited to the utmost by the charming pressure which his member exerted upon its sensitive root. 'No, no, the little charmer is not quite big enough yet to do any harm, he is just the size to give me as much pleasure as he will give you. So don't be afraid to do anything you like, and I shall do my best to help you!'

Encouraged by this, he commenced operations which I seconded and with all my might. At first he pushed backwards and forwards, gently and regularly, and I had no difficulty in keeping time with him, but after a little he became so excited and thrust followed thrust with such velocity and so irregularly that I found it quite impossible to keep in unison with him, and could only aid his frantic efforts by the compression of the muscles upon his raging champion, which I exerted whenever he gave me an opportunity by making a more prolonged thrust then usual within me. In the meantime his panting sobs and sighs bore testimony to the excess of his enjoyment and the near approach of the voluptuous crisis, which was speedily announced by an exclamation, 'Oh, goodness, oh!' I felt my delightful invader pressed into me with all his force, as if he wished his whole body could follow. I endeavoured to add to his delight by a few movements on my part, for he was now so overcome with pleasure as to be almost incapable of motion, and contracting the mouth of the orifice as much as I could, I pressed upon his swollen and throbbing column and strove to prolong his pleasure by delaying as long as possible the passage of the precious liquid through it, which was now bursting from him in furious jets. I succeeded in this so well that he has often told me since that in all the amorous encounters he has subsequently been engaged in, and they are not a few, he has never enjoyed such delicious sensations as he did on this occasion when he first felt the ravishing delight of his pleasure-giving member being completely engulfed within, and compressed by, the magical circle of living flesh.

After he had lain quiet for a little while, I felt his somewhat attenuated weapon slip out of me. He then turned himself round, presenting his buttocks to me and, still keeping his hold on my member which he had maintained during all his raptures, he gently drew me round also, nothing unwilling, and presenting his captive at the entrance to its destined prison, he opened the lips of his orifice as much as he could, and tried to get him in.

I was amused and delighted with his eagerness about it, but fearful of hurting him, I did not attempt to force my way in, until he asked me why I did not assist him in getting it farther in. I said simply because I was afraid that, as he had not tried it before, I might hurt him the first time, but that if he would allow me to try, I would endeavour to do it with as little suffering to him as possible. He at once told me to do anything I liked, that he could not expect me to allow him to enjoy himself within me again unless he reciprocated the pleasure and that he would willingly suffer any amount of pain to be permitted again to taste the delight he had already felt. I was in no way averse to take him at his word and accordingly set to work. As he gave me every facility, I was enabled with the aid of a little cold cream to make my way in with less difficulty than I had expected. My first penetration no doubt hurt him a little, but he bore it manfully and urged me to proceed till, to my infinite delight, I was fairly lodged within him up to the hilt. The avenue was as tight and delightful as possible, but it was of that charming elasticity which yielded sufficiently to admit the invader, and at the same time pressed upon him with that degree of force which occasioned the most consummate voluptuous gratifications. As soon as I was fairly in, all annoyance seemed fairly at an end and, judging from the rise of his thermometer which I held in my hand, there succeeded an increase of the pleasure heat which I had hardly anticipated. The result was that eagerly availing himself of the lessons I had given him, he set to work so deliciously and exerted himself so much to promote my pleasure that in spite of my efforts to prolong the enjoyment, he drew down from me in a very few minutes the first flow that had saturated his virgin premises.

After some little fondling of each other he again wished to repeat the operation. I told him I was afraid of his exerting himself too much, and proposed that we should put it off till morning, but he would not be satisfied with this, and urged me to comply by appealing to an argument the strength and beauty of which I could not withstand. Again this fascinating charmer was plunged into my interior with the same lascivious results and again I was rewarded for my compliance by the full enjoyment of his delicious charms, and after we had each thus attained again to the height of felicity we fell asleep locked in a close embrace.

I awoke early in the morning before he did, and I delighted myself with a view of all his naked charms while he still slumbered. I was unwilling to awaken him even to satisfy my own raging desires inflamed by the sight of such beauty, for I saw that his lovely champion was already raising his head proudly aloft, as fiercely as if he had not undergone any fatigue on the previous night, and I was convinced that if he once awoke, nothing would prevent him from at once commencing and continuing the delightful game till it was time to appear at breakfast.

I therefore resolved to keep quiet as long as possible, and creeping gently as close to him as I could, I placed my throbbing weapon in the hollow between his buttocks, and in that delicious position remained quiet until he awoke. When he did open his eyes, he turned his head round, and finding how he was situated and that I had been awake for some time, he scolded me for wasting so much valuable time, and while he took hold of and insinuated my pleasure-giver into the appropriate niche with which it was in such close contact, he vowed that he was much disposed to punish me by not allowing him to enter.

The joys of the previous evening were repeated. He in his turn penetrated into my interior, and revelled in the same lascivious enjoyment. After we had each thus allayed our fires a little by a copious discharge, we proceeded to a minute examination of our respective persons, while I was highly delighted with the unrestrained exhibition of such charms as have seldom fallen under my notice.

I found that he was not less struck and pleased with what I in return placed at his disposal. Anything of the kind he had previously seen had been of boys of his own age, and this merely by stealth when he had no opportunity of making minute observations. My somewhat more mature proportions, occasioned by the difference of a few years in our ages, were therefore fully appreciated and drew from him the warmest encomiums and the most luxurious caresses.

While Frank and I were thus agreeably occupied in a minute investigation of each other's charms, I reverted to

43

what had fallen from him the previous evening, and asked if he really meant to say that his sister was in the habit of visiting him after he had gone to bed.

'Not now,' he replied, 'I only wish she did, and I would soon repay her the lessons she used to give me. Do you know it was she who first taught me how to do anything in this way?'

I expressed my surprise and curiosity to know what had occurred between them, and he at once proceeded to enlighten me, saying that from the kindness I had shown him he was sure he need have no reserve with me.

'It was,' he said, 'just last holidays when I had returned from school, that our first amusement began. We then slept in the same rooms we now occupy, and as some of my younger brothers were in the room where you are, I used often to lock the door at night to prevent them from coming in and tormenting me. Laura used generally to come to bed before her aunt. She somehow ascertained that I shut myself up in my room and probably imagined that I was better informed on certain subjects than I really was.

'One evening on which there were some old people at dinner who were likely to occupy our aunt's attention and keep her up late, Laura said to me that she was tired of the party in the drawing room, but that she was not inclined to sleep, and that if I left the door open between our rooms she would come and sit with me for a while. I sat up for some time, expecting to hear her come to her room, but at length I grew tired of waiting, undressed, and went to bed. I suspected she must have crept softly to her own room and waited there without my being aware of it till this took place, for I had hardly got into bed and put out the candle when I heard her come in. She came to the bedside and inquired in a low voice if I was awake. On my answering her, she said we had better not talk loud in case of disturbing the young people in the next room. She sat down by the bedside and leaned over me, putting an arm round my neck and kissing me warmly. Then, putting her hand under the bed-clothes, she began to caress my naked bosom. This seemed a little strange to me, but very pleasant. And it was still more agreeable when, putting my arm round her neck, I found that she also was undressed and had nothing but her nightshift and a dressing gown which was quite open at the front. This she accounted for by saying she must be ready to slip into bed if she heard her aunt coming.

'The touch of her naked breasts, with their full, round form, quite delighted me, and it was while playing with them that the first voluptuous sensations were awakened within me. I had previously been sometimes surprised, especially on awakening in the morning, to find a certain little gentleman quite hard and stiff, and had been at a loss to ascertain what was the cause. And I was now still more surprised that as I played with her soft yielding globes, the same effect occurred, but although the sensation was most agreeable, I was too ignorant regarding such matters to be able to connect the cause with the effect. Laura continued to kiss and play with me for some time, and at last I became aware that while with one hand she caressed me, the other was employed in some movement about her own person, the object of which I did not understand and did not think of investigating. The effect, however, seemed to be pleasant to her, for her kisses and caresses increased in ardour till at last with a heavy sigh they ceased at once; and she remained for a few minutes perfectly still. Then after another kiss she said she was afraid her aunt might come and find her away. So making me promise to say nothing of her visit she left me.

'Our interview had been so agreeable to me that I pressed her to renew it on the succeeding night, which she willingly agreed to do, and somewhat of the same procedure occurred on that and several subsequent occasions. I gradually began to discover that as her caresses increased and as her hand came to wander lower down on my person the effect which was produced upon a certain part came to increase in force and to be accompanied with more pleasant sensations. This aroused a suspicion in my mind that there must be some connection between them. So one night, when my little plaything was particularly stiff, and she was very much excited, I took her hand which had never before strayed below my navel and, certainly by no means unwillingly on her part, drew it down and placed it on the throbbing object that had raised my curiosity. She made not the least objection to my making her grasp it, and after handling it for a little, she asked me what was the meaning of it and what I wanted her to do with it. I said I did not know, but that I suspected she knew better than I did, as it was only when she played with me that it became in its present state. She laughed and asked me if it gave me any pleasure for her to play with it. I told her it did, and begged of her to continue to fondle it. She complied very willingly, and then began to question me how long it was since it had commenced to get into this state and whether I had ever played with it myself, or done anything to procure myself pleasure with it. I told her that it was only of late that it had often been in the way of getting stiff, and explained how much it had been affected by her caresses. She then said she thought she might perhaps be able to procure for me still greater pleasure with it, but that it would take a little time to do so, and as she could not remain long enough that night she would come back and try what she could do on the first favourable opportunity.

'The next evening she complained of a headache and retired to bed earlier than usual. As soon as she came into my room, she lighted my candle, stripped down the bed-clothes, made me take off my nightshirt, and at once began to amuse herself with my little plaything. It swelled out and increased in size under her playful fondling to an extent that surprised me. After she had satisfied her curiosity respecting it and its appendages by a strict examination of every part, she took it in her hand and began to rub it up and down. She then put out the candle, so that I did not see what was probably the

46

case – while endeavouring to procure me pleasure, she was at the same time operating upon herself for the same agreeable purpose. I certainly very much enjoyed her performance upon my sensitive article, but still I felt as if something was wanting, and I was greatly disappointed when as usual she sunk almost fainting on my bosom and ceased her efforts.

'After a little she recovered herself and said she was afraid I was still too young to be able to enjoy the full pleasure of what she had been doing, but that she would try again the following night. Still two or three nights passed without anything occurring to heighten my enjoyment.

'By this time I had begun to express some curiosity with regard to her person and to wish to be allowed to extend my researches over it as freely as her hands roved over mine. With some little difficulty I prevailed on her to remove her dressing gown and nightshift and stretch herself naked on the bed beside me. I had been aware from what I had seen of some girls that there was a considerable difference in our formation, but I was astonished at first on finding her centre-part so thickly shaded with hair. I, quite delighted with its beauty, was soon tempted to get my fingers between the moist ruby lips of the charming little slit which I discovered within the curly forest, and to begin to explore its recess. The sensitive little organ I found within so closely resembling, though on a smaller scale, my own organ of pleasure, did not escape my observation, as wakened up by my lascivious touches it darted its little head out from its hiding-place. It was not long before I discovered that this invasion of her inmost recesses occasioned Laura the greatest delight. She seemed at first to hesitate a little, but summing up courage she took hold of my hand and, inserting my fingers within the warmly moist cavity, made me move it up and down within her. At the same time she grasped my weapon and rubbed it backwards and forwards more rapidly and more forcibly than she had ever done before. I felt greatly excited and continued the titillating movements of my finger within her with the greatest zest, until I saw her stretch her legs out and sink backwards on the bed sobbing violently, while with quick hurried movements of her buttocks she responded to every thrust I made in her inflamed interior. These violent emotions only lasted a few seconds, and then I felt something wet apparently issue from her, trickle over my fingers and down her thighs. She still retained her grasp of my machine, which I felt throbbing and burning more fiercely than ever and giving me more pleasure than I had ever previously experienced, though in her crisis of delight she had ceased to operate upon it. I now begged for her not to stop, but to continue her employment which afforded me so much delight. Suspecting what was indeed the case, that the sight of her charms and of the enjoyment she had undergone had stirred me up to an unwonted pitch of desire which might perhaps be attended with a happy result, she good-naturedly resumed her efforts, and every succeeding movement of her hand upon the throbbing and inflamed member evidently added intensely to the flame that consumed me. She persevered until she had produced the desired result, and I saw a drop or two of white liquid burst from the inflamed point, while at the same time a most delicious sensation pushed through the part affected and from thence seemed to thrill through my whole frame, as overcome with the exquisite delight I fell back upon the bed, she kissing me tenderly and congratulating me on having at length attained the powers of a man; then she left me to my repose.

'After this we omitted no opportunity that was afforded us of amusing ourselves together in the same way. My ignorance on the subject, however, prevented me from thinking of carrying our enjoyment farther, and though doubtless she knew better, she allowed me to return to school without enlightening me any farther. She made me promise two things, first that I was not to indulge myself in any repetition of our pastimes until we met again, and secondly not to say anything to my school-fellows regarding such subjects. I cannot say that I kept my promise on either point. I tried as well as I could to do so with regard to the first, but I could not help occasionally breaking through. But my curiosity was too much excited by our late proceedings not to endeavour to ascertain how some of my elder companions felt regarding such subjects. On sounding them cautiously I discovered that some of them were better informed on such affairs than I was, and from their revelations I became aware of the amount of pleasure I had lost through my want of knowledge to avail myself of it. Since then I have endeavoured to prevail on her to afford me an opportunity of repeating our amusements, but she always puts me off, laughing and saying that I am grown too old for her to allow me to play these tricks now, so that I never have been able to show her what a change had taken place in the size of her old acquaintance or to prove to her how much pleasure I am sure it could now give her.'

This detail produced such an exciting effect upon both of our organs of pleasure that we were obliged again to quench our raging fires in each other's interiors. In the course of the mutual operation I questioned him as to whether, if he had an opportunity, he would like to repeat his former amusements with Laura and even carry them further. He said at once it would be most delightful to do so, and nothing would give him greater pleasure. Then referring to her close neighbour-hood to us and to her aunt's approaching departure, he said that there would be such a capital opportunity for our all enjoying ourselves together, if she could only be persuaded to agree to it, that he was determined to try whether he could not persuade her to renew their meetings, and he even showed me a key to the door leading into her room which he had got made on purpose to enable him to have access to her.

His story had somewhat enlightened me as to Laura's ideas, and I could now understand to some degree her not feeling so much annoyed as I had been at Frank's arrival. I strongly suspected that rather than be deprived of her favourite amusement, she would not object to his again being a participator in it. I thought it better, however, not to say anything to him at present regarding my intimacy with her until I had ascertained what her intentions really were. After mutually agreeing that we were both to endeavour to prevail on her to join in our sports, and that if one succeeded he was to do all he could for the benefit of the other, we went down to breakfast.

I had an opportunity sooner than I expected of coming to an explanation with Laura. She had told me that she could not meet me that morning at the summer house, but in the course of the forenoon she found she could get away for an hour, and she gave me the usual signal for me to repair there. When, as she was accustomed to do, she opened my trousers and uncovered her little darling and proceeded to give him his usual caress before introducing him into his nest, her quick eye at once discovered that he was not in his ordinary trim to satisfy her desires. With a flushed cheek, she looked me full in the face, and asked what was the reason of this and what I had been about to occasion such a state of things.

I was very well pleased to have such a good opportunity of coming to the point, and I at once answered that, having been deprived of the pleasure of seeing her in the morning and despairing of being able to accomplish a meeting with her that day, I had been reduced to the necessity of seeking consolation in the embraces of one whose charms put me so much in mind of her that I had almost believed it was her in reality and had been tempted to exceed the limits I had intended to have placed upon myself.

She inquired with some heat and astonishment what I meant. But she blushed scarlet when I replied that Frank and I had been rehearsing some of her lessons. She was at first rather annoyed at what I told her; but when I explained to her that I had not made Frank aware of what had passed between us until I was sure of her approbation and that his reason for confiding in me was the hope of my being of use in enabling him to obtain the bliss he so much coveted – of again regaling himself in her charms – she was quite appeased.

I had little difficulty in discerning that she was highly delighted with the glowing description I gave of his youthful charms and especially of the size and prowess of her old acquaintance. I dwelt on this and on the necessity there was of taking him into our confidence, and even making him a partner in our amusements, unless we were to give them up entirely, for there could be no doubt if we went on that he would soon discover the footing we were on. Although I could not get her to say that she would consent to this, I was tolerably well satisfied she would make no great opposition. I therefore ceased to urge the point, telling her that she must leave it to me to arrange matters with Frank, if I found it was necessary, and that I would take care not to commit her more than was absolutely requisite.

We had continued to caress each other during this conversation and her charms producing their usual effect upon me I was soon able to point out to her the flourishing condition of her favourite.

I exerted myself notwithstanding my previous night's work to show her that it had not quite exhausted me; and at length she left me quite reconciled by the result of three vigorous encounters.

When Frank came to me that night he was somewhat surprised at the state of my rather enervated champion, which he with great glee contrasted with the vigorous condition of his own. But he was still more surprised when I frankly confessed that I could not attempt to cope with him on that occasion, and explained the cause from which the deficiency arose. He was greatly delighted to learn the footing on which I stood with Laura, and at once concluded that she would not be able to resist the temptation of adding to her enjoyment by making him participate in it. I quite agreed with him, but at the same time I told him the objection she had made and that it would probably be necessary to devise some plan by which at least the appearance of her not

51

voluntarily complying with his desires might be kept up.

After some deliberation on this subject, occasionally interrupted by a renewal of our previous evening's amusements, in which, however, I generally allowed my young friend to take the more active share, we arranged our plan which was carried into effect in this manner.

Laura was now afraid to venture to the summer house every morning, so we had few opportunities of meeting. But ascertaining that her mother and her aunt were going two days afterwards to pay a visit at a distance, which would occupy them the whole forenoon, I arranged with her that if she were left alone, she should come to my room where I would be waiting for her. I then arranged with Frank that at breakfast he should say he was going to take a ride to call upon a companion in the neighbourhood, but that instead of doing so he should conceal himself in a closet in my room and upon my giving a certain signal he should make a noise which would lead to his discovery without it appearing that I knew he was there.

Everything happened as I anticipated. As soon as the carriage drove off with her mother, Laura came to my room, where I was awaiting her. Saying that it seemed an age since I had had the opportunity of fully enjoying the sight and touch of all her charms, I at once stripped myself quite naked and proceeded to perform the same operation upon her. As she enjoyed this as much as I did, she made no objection whatever, and even assisted in getting rid of her clothes as fast as possible. I placed her in several different postures, in order to allow the delighted boy to enjoy the voluptuous sensations I was sure her charms would produce upon him, and then proceeded to the final enjoyment. When this had been completed to our mutual satisfaction, I again displayed all her attractions, and when by kisses and caresses and lascivious touches I had again roused her desires for a repetition of the encounter, I made the agreed-on signal to Frank. He immediately responded by pushing down some article of furniture. Laura started up, exclaiming, 'Good heavens, what is that? Can anyone be there?'

I jumped out of the bed and seized a pistol which was lying on the dressing table and opened the door saying I would take good care to silence any intruder so that he should never be able to tell upon us. On opening the door and disclosing Frank, I exclaimed, 'So it is you, Master Peeping Tom. Well, it is lucky it is only you, for anyone else would have had a good chance of having a bullet through his head. But I shall deal somewhat differently with you. Don't suppose, however, you are to get off unpunished for thus stealing in upon us. I see there is a good rod here, and you shall have a sound flogging for your impertinence and curiosity. So strip instantly and remember the longer you are about it the more severe your punishment will be.'

Frank appeared nothing loth to submit to the proposed infliction and with my assistance was soon as naked as we were.

All this time I watched Laura closely to observe how she was affected by our proceedings. At first she had been dreadfully alarmed, but on finding it was only Frank she was quite aware she was perfectly safe. As I proceeded to strip him, and disclosed his exquisite figure and symmetrical proportions, she evidently became much interested, and when at last I drew his shirt over his head and revealed the full contour of his body with his delicious charmer standing fully erect and exhibiting its rosy head completely developed, I could see a flash of pleasure and delight steal over her lovely features and impart still greater animation to her sparkling eyes. Convinced that I might now proceed to any extremities I said, 'Now, Laura, you must assist me to punish this young rogue properly.'

I then gave her the rod, and sitting down on the side of the bed, I placed him across my knees and turned up his beautiful posteriors to her. She instantly entered into the sport and gave him two or three cuts with the birch which, though not very severe, were quite sufficient to give him an excuse for tossing his legs about and exhibiting all his charms in the most voluptuous manner possible, in which I gave him every assistance in my power. After this playful enjoyment had been continued for some time, I said to Laura that she was too gentle with him and did not punish him half so severely as he deserved, and proposed that she should change places with me and let me take the rod. She laughingly assented and asked me in what position she was to hold him for me. I told her the best plan would be to do as they flogged the boys at school, and I would show her how it was done. Making her lean forward upon the bed, I placed him behind her, and putting his arms over her shoulders, I made her catch hold of his hands, telling her to hold them fast. She did as I directed, while I applied a few lashes to his plump, handsome posteriors which, as I expected, made him cling closely to Laura, bringing his instrument into direct contact with her buttocks, against which it beat furiously, as if eager to effect an entrance somewhere.

I said, 'Ah, I see you have got a very unruly little gentleman there, I must try if we can't hold him fast also.' And at the same time I inserted it between her thighs and again inflicted a few blows.

The near approach of his furious weapon to the seat of pleasure caused him to make fierce efforts to endeavour to penetrate it, and I could no longer resist the imploring glances he cast upon me, expressive of his urgent desire that I should enable him to complete his enjoyment. So making Laura rest her belly on the bed and stretch her legs as far asunder as possible so as to afford him a fair entrance from behind, I loosened her hold of his arms so far as to enable him to stoop down sufficiently low, and then taking hold of his flaming weapon I guided it into the heaven which I felt was burning with desire and eager to receive it. Laura at once accommodated herself to all his proceedings and finding that her hold of his hands rather obstructed his progress, she loosened it, and they were soon transferred to her splendid swelling globes, and then, as he became more and more excited in the hot struggle, were firmly clasped round her waist so as to bring their bodies into the closest possible contact. Animated by the delicious scene before my eyes the fiery impatience of my excited organ of pleasure could no longer be restrained. I threw myself on the lovely young man and almost at the first thrust was plunged up to the hilt in the delicious buttocks which he thus so temptingly exposed to my eager assault.

Once engulfed I had nothing to do but to keep my place and leave to the energetic struggles of the other two combatants the task of bringing the warfare to a successful termination.

After a hard fight, during which the utmost endeavours of both parties seemed to be to try which should be vanquished soonest, it terminated in a drawn battle.

And as I contributed at the same time my share of the spoil, poor Frank's beautiful little balls of delight were quite inundated both before and behind with the stream which flowed from himself and me and which mingled with the first tribute his manly prowess had drawn down from woman and poured in torrents along his thighs. The dear boy was so overcome with the delight that I thought at first he must have fainted, but I soon discovered it was only the swoon of pleasure. Raising him up in my arms, as soon as I could disengage my unruly member from the pleasant quarters it still clung too, I laid him on the bed by the side of Laura who was not in much better condition and stood equally in need of my assistance.

It is wonderful, however, how soon one recovers from such exhaustion, and in a few minutes they were both as lively as ever and were actively engaged in the mutual contemplation of each other's exquisite charms. This pleasant proceeding was enlivened by an animated discussion regarding the alteration and improvement which each of them discovered the other's beauties had undergone since they had last been submitted to their mutual inspection, and it cannot be doubted that Laura was greatly delighted to witness the change in size of the pretty little champion to which she had given the first lesson. All this, of course, produced the usual effect upon us, and Frank seeing that I was quite ready to renew the combat proposed to resign Laura to me. I fancied, however, that they would like repetition of their previous engagement, and he was evidently perfectly able to renew it, for, indeed, the wanton boy had been so wound up by the preliminary scene that his former encounter had produced hardly any relaxing effect upon his lovely weapon. I therefore drew him upon the not unwilling Laura, and again guiding the fiery courser into the lists of pleasure, had the satisfaction of seeing them once more commence the amorous encounter, which proceeded to the ordinary happy result, evidently to the great delight of both parties.

Frank, revelling in the blissful conjunction of every part of their naked bodies, clasped Laura round the neck and imprinted burning kisses upon her lovely lips, while his rampant steed plunged violently backwards and forwards in the abyss of pleasure and his charming buttocks bounded and quivered with the excess of wanton delight. Greatly interested in watching the delightful encounter, I endeavoured to promote their enjoyment by tickling and playing with them in the most sensitive places, till their excitement reached its height and they both sunk down in the swoon of pleasure.

Laura had no sooner recovered a little from the effects of this engagement, than Frank insisted on seeing me perform the same pleasant operation in which he had just been engaged. Nothing loth, I immediately humoured his fancy, getting upon Laura, who was still lying on her back in the bed. The lascivious and not yet exhausted boy had no sooner got us fairly placed and my weapon inserted in Laura's sheath and set to work, than I felt him separate our legs so as to enable him to kneel down between them behind us. Having established his position satisfactorily, he instantly plunged his still rampant champion into my rear, producing in me the most rapturous sensations, which soon caused me in conjunction with Laura to die away in bliss before he was ready to join our sacrifice.

Finding that he was determined to complete his third pleasing operation, I proposed that he should change his position and take up my place in Laura's palace of pleasure and allow me again to stimulate him in the rear, and assist him to attain his object. He highly approved of this proposal, and immediately took up his position in Laura's arms, while, getting behind him and inserting my weapon in his delicious sheath, I proceeded to render him the same agreeable service he had just done me. This speedily had the desired effect, and a delicious emission from all the three parties brought our undertaking to a most successful and satisfactory conclusion.

By this time, Laura for once had had enough to satisfy her, and we separated, sadly grudging the loss of the two days which were still to pass before the departure of her aunt would admit to a renewal of our joys in security. We faithfully proposed on our part that we should be abstinent in the meantime with the view of being the better able to enjoy ourselves thoroughly when the happy time for our all again meeting together should arrive. Upon the whole, with the assistance of an occasional solace from her in the summer house, when an opportunity afforded, we kept our promise tolerably well, though as Frank would insist on coming to my bed, and we could neither of us refrain from indulging in a sight of each other's charms, it was sometimes a hard struggle to restrain our desires.

At length Miss Middleton's departure enabled us to give free course to all our wanton inclinations, and night after night my room was the scene of a repetition of the most exquisite and voluptuous enjoyments it is possible to conceive. When our exhausted frames could no longer furnish us with the means of indulging in the performance of our soul-stirring rites, we were never tired of gazing on and caressing the delicious forms which were constantly exhibited without reserve for the delectation and amusement of one another, for we all seemed to feel that our own delight was heightened by aiding to promote the happiness of the others. We had no secrets from Laura; in fact, she had witnessed with delight the pleasures which Frank and I mutually conferred upon each other. On one occasion when she was disqualified from joining in our amusements, she watched Frank and me stripping and enjoying by ourselves the pleasures she was unable to participate in.

The evident delight they afforded us affected her so greatly that she declared she must try the effect of the same operation upon herself. Accordingly, the next night she insisted upon us both operating on her at the same time. Frank offered to me the choice of routes. But as I was aware that he had often contemplated with great pleasure the idea of opening up the new way, which he thought would be peculiarly well suited to his yet somewhat undeveloped proportions, I at once gave him the precedence. I told him that, as I had already had one victory over a maiden citadel, it was only fair that he should enjoy the next and that it was better he should do so, as in all probability he would obtain it with less suffering to the conquered fair one than if my larger battering ram were at first introduced. Laura quite approved of this arrangement. Having all stripped quite naked, I laid myself down in the bed at full length and then drew her upon me, making her place herself so as to bring her cavity just over the stiff pole which was standing up ready to enter it. She herself inserted and adjusted it in the most satisfactory manner. When she was quite impaled upon me and firmly fastened by the wedge being fairly driven home in her, Frank got between her legs on his knees, and with lance in hand, proceeded to insert it in her hinder cavity. Being, however, his first attempt at storming a maiden fortress, he was not very expert at it, and

58

the coveted way proving very narrow and confined, it was not without some difficulty he effected his object. The obstacles, however, only increased the ardour of his desires, and, with the assistance of a little cold cream, they were at length happily surmounted, and his weapon forced its way into the interior of the citadel. During this time I endeavoured to keep as quiet as possible, and as Frank's efforts occasioned her some pain, Laura also remained nearly motionless, only exerting herself a little occasionally to humour his movements and assist him in effecting an entrance. As soon, however, as I found from his exclamation of delight that his weapon had overcome all resistance and was as fully embedded in the lascivious, fleshy sheath as mine was, I began at first gently and quietly, and then more rapidly and vigorously, to join in the combat, heaving my buttocks up and down and urging the lusty pole backwards and forwards in its delicious quarters, only pausing now and then to receive and return the burning kisses which Laura, now rendered quite frantic with the double enjoyment stimulating her both before and behind, showered upon me. I soon found that any further efforts on my part were quite unnecessary. Maddened by the novel excitement, Laura heaved and thrust alternately, displacing and replacing the sturdy instruments above and below, and declaring she really knew not which of them afforded her the greatest delight. I, therefore, confined myself to favouring her movements so as to give them the greatest possible effect, till at last with her eyes flashing fire and her whole body panting and heaving with the excess of her emotion, she almost shouted out, 'Oh, heavens, this is too much!' Her grasp round me slackened, and she sunk entranced on my bosom, while Frank and I responded to her call, and a few frantic heaves on both our parts served to cause our rivers of delight to flow into her where, mingling with her own flood, they somewhat served to calm our over-excited senses.

It was some time before Laura came to herself, but when

she did she was delighted to find that we still retained our respective positions within her. On my inquiring whether they felt disposed for a renewal of the combat in a similar manner, they both declared with the most impassioned caresses that nothing would give them greater delight.

Telling Frank that as the entrance to both fortresses was now well lubricated, we might venture to carry on the warfare more boldly without the risk of doing any damage, I desired him to keep time with me and thrust his weapon as far in and out as he could at each heave, first alternately with me and then on a given signal both together.

At the same time I advised Laura to remain quiet and try what would be the effect of our efforts. The result far surpassed her expectations. When, after heaving alternately for some little time, I gave Frank the signal and we made a simultaneous thrust together, burying both our weapons as far as they would go within the soft yielding flesh, she exclaimed, 'Oh, this is exquisite, it could not possibly be more heavenly.' We continued this mode of action for some time, alternately changing from one variety to another, while she responded merely by twisting and wriggling her buttocks, and in turn compressing and squeezing the darling object before or behind, which for the moment affected her senses the more powerfully. Gradually, however, she became too much animated to adhere to any settled plan, and she could not refrain from meeting and returning our lusty efforts to promote her enjoyment. This only animated us to fresh exertions in which we were so successful that we were soon rewarded by as overpowering an overflow of bliss as before.

As soon as it was over, she insisted on laying us both out at full length on the bed quite naked, bring our organs of pleasure so close together that she could caress them at the same time, and placing herself upon us so that her mouth came in contact with them. In this position she remained for a long time – kissing, caressing, and sucking the instruments of delight and thanking us in the warmest manner for the excessive joy we had given her until her luscious caresses, exciting us almost to madness, forced us again to allay the irritation produced on our burning weapons by again bringing them into her delightful sheaths.

In such exquisite amusements a few weeks passed rapidly away without any interruption to our joys, when we were startled by learning from Laura that there was a derangement of the usual symptoms which she feared indicated pregnancy. This greatly alarmed us, for trusting to our youth we had had no fear on this subject. I lost no time in consulting an eminent London surgeon, but his reply was that the symptoms were usual in cases of pregnancy, but that they were not infallible signs of it, as they sometimes occurred from other causes. It was, however, obvious that some arrangement must be made to provide for the occurrence of the possible event. I, of course, told Laura that if it should turn out as she feared, we must make up our minds to run off together and getting up a story of her having been previously privately married, keep out of the way until the noise of the affair blew over. This plan, however, did not meet her approbation. She said that whatever might really have been the case, everyone would at once say from the difference in our ages that she must have seduced me and that she would never be able to show her face again in society, and that moreover she could not think of inflicting such a penalty on me as to saddle me for life with a wife older than myself, when she had been as much to blame in the matter as I had.

After a great deal of consideration I ventured to hint whether her best plan would not be to accept Sir Charles Tracy, marry him at once, and get the ceremony over without delay, so that if a child did come, there might be at least the lapse of six months to admit of the possibility of his being the father.

I must here explain that Sir Charles had been an almost constant resident at the Hall ever since my arrival, and was evidently looked upon by the family as a suitor. He was a young man of about twenty-seven, of large fortune, tall, handsome, and well made, not particularly clever, but almost the best-tempered and most good-natured person I ever met. His object in remaining so long was quite obvious. Although she would never admit it, I had all along fancied that Laura liked him; but since I had become so intimate with her, she certainly had shown more coldness towards him than she did on my first arrival.

At first, Laura said this plan would never do. But, as we could devise nothing else, on my pressing her a little on the subject she admitted that before I came she had made up her mind to accept him if he proposed, but that she was afraid to do so now for two reasons: first, she feared he might discover on his first attack that someone had had access before him to the sanctuary of love and secondly, from the dread that in the event of a child coming before the usual time he might denounce her and turn her adrift.

I considered a little, and then asked her whether if these difficulties could be got over she would still be disposed to marry him.

She said it was no use thinking of it, but that if it were not for the objections she had mentioned, she certainly would, as she thought she could live happily with him.

I then told her that as to the first objection she might set her mind perfectly at ease, for from what I had already seen of Sir Charles, his instrument I knew was so much larger than anything that had found its way into her and he would find so much difficulty in getting it in for the first time that he would never suspect any intruder had been before him, and that if, as she easily might, she insisted in the operation being performed in the dark, I could supply her with a contrivance by which a little red liquid might be applied so as to produce the natural appearance of an effusion of blood. Then as to the second objection, I told her I thought there would be little fear of his making any complaint at least in public on the

62

subject, if she had the power to hold out to him that she could bring forward a matter which it would be equally unpleasant for him to have disclosed.

She said that in such a case the matter might perhaps be arranged, but she could not imagine how she was to obtain such a hold over him.

I told her I thought she might leave that to me. I then explained to her that Sir Charles had taken a fancy to me on my arrival, and had shown me every kindness and attention, evidently wishing to be on an intimate footing with me.

The poor fellow no doubt was in an awkward predicament. Inflamed by the constant sight of the charms of Laura, of whom he was greatly enamoured, he was afraid to console himself in the arms of any of the women in the neighbourhood for fear his infidelity might come to her knowledge, and unable wholly to restrain his desire to give vent in some manner to his pent-up passions, he had made some overtures to me of which I clearly understood the meaning, though with Laura, Betsy, and Frank on my hands, I had quite enough to do in that way, and consequently I had pretended not to understand his intentions. I now suggested to Laura that by complying with his wishes I might get him to come to my room where she and Frank would have an opportunity of seeing us enjoy each other, so that if at any future period he should accuse her of infidelity prior to her marriage, she might retort upon him.

Laura was quite satisfied that, if this could be accomplished, she would be perfectly safe; as with his good temper she said she had little doubt, even in case of the worst we dreaded occurring, she would be able to persuade him that it would be for the interests of both that he should keep quiet, seeing she had such a hold over him. She now admitted that she really was fond of him, though her curiosity and my boldness had lately enabled me to gain the advantage over him, and I easily drew from her that she did not like him the less for the report I had made of his evident ability to perform satisfactorily in the battles of Venus. I therefore told her that, though I was afraid that the performance of the instrument that would probably afford the greatest pleasure to her might prove to be martyrdom to me, I was prepared to undergo it for her sake, and we signed and sealed the agreements in our usual happy way.

As I have always found that where a thing is once determined on it is better to lose no time in carrying it into execution, I set to work immediately. I dressed for dinner that day sooner than usual, and about half an hour before the ordinary dinner hour, I made my way to Sir Charles' room, taking with me an amorous work he had lent me and making a pretext of wishing to borrow another. When he found who it was that knocked at the door he asked me to come in, saying that he wanted to see me as he had that day received a packet from town with some things he had ordered down for me. He then told his servant to lay out some things for him, and that he would not be required further. As soon as the servant had left the room, he took from a drawer a large parcel, and selecting a packet of drawings, told me to sit down and amuse myself with them while he finished dressing.

This was coming to the point even sooner than I had anticipated, but as it was just the opening I wanted, I sat down and began to examine the drawings which consisted of a most beautifully executed series of voluptuous designs. When he had dressed himself, all except his coat and waistcoat (and he was a very few minutes about it), he came and leaned over me, looking at the drawings and making observations upon them. After we had gone over them, he said there were some more which he liked still better and he hoped I would be equally well pleased with them. He went to the drawer for them, while I rose up to lay aside those we had been looking at. He selected two packets, and then coming back to the easy chair in which I had been sitting, he sat down, and wished to draw me on his knee.

64

This, however, I did not allow, but I sat down on the arm of the chair allowing him to put his arm round my waist. He exhibited some more illustrations of luscious scenes, many of which were new to me, and I did not attempt to conceal the effect which was produced upon me, while I told him, which was the case, that I had never seen anything of the kind more beautifully designed and executed. I could see that he was watching the impression made not only on my face but also on another part of my person, which had now become somewhat prominent. He seemed satisfied with this, and then opened the other packet, which was a series of drawings executed by a first-rate artist in the most admirable style delineating the seduction of a beautiful boy of about sixteen by another handsome youth a few years older. Every scene in the progress was illustrated by an appropriate and admirably drawn portrait of the two characters, commencing with taking him on his knee and impressing the first amorous kiss; the laying of his hand upon the organ of pleasure; the maiden bashfulness of first feeling the naked weapon grasped by a strange hand; the first starting out of the beautiful object on the trousers being unloosened; the full development of all its beauties on their being removed; the drawing his bridle over the fiery little head of the charger; the playing with the beautiful little appendices; the opening the thighs to get a glimpse of the seat of pleasure behind; the turning him round to obtain a full view of the exquisite hindquarters; the first exposure to his gaze of the second actor in the scene of pleasure; the making him caress and play with it; the complete exposure of all their naked charms as their shirts are drawn over their heads; the close embrace as they strain each other in their arms; the turning him round to present the altar for the sacrifice; the entrance; the combat; the extasy; the offering the recompensing pleasure; the introducing the virgin weapon for the first time; the ardour of the first enjoyment; the first tribute and the mutual embrace of thanks as they kissed and caressed each other's organs of pleasure after the work happily was accomplished. All these were depicted with a beauty and a truth to nature that forcibly reminded me of my own sweet experience of similar enjoyment on my first initiation in the secrets of pleasure. As I gazed with admiration upon them, he could not help observing how much I was interested, and was no doubt encouraged to think, as I intended he should be, that there would be little objection on my part of his proceeding to enact a similar scene. His hand gradually slipped down over my stiffly distended weapon. I made a little faint resistance, but gradually allowed him, without much difficulty, to handle and feel it, to unloosen my trousers and make it appear on the stage. He had no sooner got possession of it, than he loaded it with kisses and caresses, declaring that he had never seen anything to surpass it in beauty. He had not much more difficulty in loosening my braces and completely removing my trousers so as to give him a full opportunity of seeing and handling my naked person.

I affected to be so much engrossed with the pictures as not to observe that he had not only done this, but had also drawn down his own trousers and raised up his shirt displaying his magnificent weapon, until taking my hand he tried to make me grasp – for my fingers could not meet round it – by far the most splendid and largest champion I had ever met with, one which, indeed, I have never seen surpassed. He seemed much amused by my surprised exclamation. 'Oh, goodness, what a monster,' and, laughing, asked if I had never seen one so large before. But on my expressing my wonder that he should ever get it into a woman at all he seemed to be a little apprehensive that I might be too much frightened to allow it to enter where he wished it should go, and he tried to persuade me that after all there was not so very great a difference between it and mine.

In truth I had begun to be somewhat terrified on the subject and to wish at least to delay the operation, if it must be undergone, until it could be effected in a place where the object desired could be secured. I knew that in a few minutes the dinner bell would ring, and I therefore determined to temporise as long as possible and escape on the present occasion by holding out hopes of his attaining his object on a more favourable opportunity.

But I found that it was easier to make the resolution than to keep it. His evident passion for me and the means he adopted to excite me to an ardour equal to his own – keeping up a titillatory friction over the most sensitive points of my body – soon produced their effect, and in spite of my resolution, I could not make any effort to oppose him. Having drawn me on his knees, he raised me up, and opening my buttocks and holding apart the lips of the orifice, he presented the enormous head of his charger and tried to gain admittance. He seemed to be aware that there must be considerable difficulty, and he not only anointed the parts with cold-cream, but he also refrained from attempting to force it in by any violent exertion on his part, apparently wishing that the junction should be brought about in a manner that would run less risk of occasioning me pain by my pressing gently down upon it myself. This he urgently begged me to do, and I could not withhold feeling sensible of this attention to my feelings on his part. I thought it would be hardly fair of me not to show that I was so by at least endeavouring, as far as I could, to aid in accomplishing his wishes. I therefore pressed down upon the impaling stroke with as much force as I could venture to exert, and with great difficulty and some pain did get the head fairly within the entrance. Having attained this, I desisted from my efforts for a moment and was pleased to find that the pain ceased entirely. As for him, he was perfectly enchanted and loaded me with kisses and caresses. Just then the bell announced that dinner would be on the table in five minutes. Although I had previously been anxiously expecting this announcement, I must confess I felt sorry when it did come, for I had now got so interested and excited in our proceedings that I would willingly have contributed by every means in my power, even at any sacrifice of pain, to bring the enterprise to a successful termination. But there seemed no help for it, and I turned my head round to him and said that I was afraid we must go downstairs. He caught me round the neck, pressed my lips passionately to his, and entreated me to have patience with him for a few moments; he said he would not attempt to do anything that would give me more pain, but that he was then enjoying the most transcendent pleasure from the kind assistance I had already afforded him in getting his instrument so far imbedded in the abode of bliss, and if I would only allow him to remain where he was for a few seconds longer, he would be overwhelmed with the excess of his joy and would never cease to be grateful to me for having thus contributed to it. I could not resist his appeal, seeing clearly from his excited and flashing eyes that the tempest was nearly at its height, and on the eve of bursting forth with all the fury of a torrent.

He did not attempt to force his way further in, but supporting me with his arms he wriggled and twisted his buttocks making his weapon move about within me in the most surprising and delicious manner. Wishing to gratify and assist him as far as I could, I put one hand behind and grasping as well as I could the lower part of the splendid pillar, I rubbed and squeezed it, endeavouring to increase the excitement and promote his object; then passing the other hand between my thighs, I tickled and played with the massy round globes I found just beneath my own and which instead of hanging down, pendant as at first, were now closely drawn up in their wondrous purse. He kissed me again fervently and was in the act of thanking me for my kindness in thus increasing his pleasure, when he suddenly stopped short with a passionate exclamation of a single 'Oh!' My hand, which grasped his splendid weapon, was sensible of the instant rush of the fiery liquid through it, and the next moment, I felt the warm gush driven into my entrails as if it had been forced up

68

by a pump. I continued the motion of my hand gently upon his instrument until the fit of pleasure was entirely over. Then, with some difficulty disengaging myself from the link that bound us together, I wiped the ruby head of the still rampant champion, and stooping down, first kissed it and then his lips as he still lay reclining in the chair and then proceeded to arrange my dress. He soon recovered himself and earnestly begged that I would come to his room that night that he might have an opportunity of thanking me and of endeavouring to repay, as far as he possibly could, the delicious treat I had afforded him. This, however, I would not promise to do, saying I was too much afraid of being seen when I could have no excuse for being in his room, but I allowed him to understand that I would try to devise some plan for another meeting.

I contrived to give Laura a hint before dinner that all was right and that she would get the details at night. She was so delighted with this that the distance and hauteur with which she had lately treated Sir Charles were greatly removed, and he on his part, animated by the scene which had just taken place and his victory, as he thought, over my virgin charms, was more lively and bolder than usual. So that by the end of the evening they were on a better and more familiar footing than they had ever been before. When the ladies retired to bed, Sir Charles again urged me to go to his room. I still refused, but at last I suggested that perhaps he might come to me early the next morning, as this would be less liable to suspicion, for if anyone saw him we might go out immediately together, when it would be supposed he had only come for the purpose of calling me, while if he was not observed, he might remain for a time with me. Of course, that night I explained to Laura and Frank all that had passed, and we contrived to make two apertures in the partition wall of the closet between Frank's room and mine, from which they would have an uninterrupted view of the scene of operations.

The next morning I heard Sir Charles open my door, but I

lay quiet as if still asleep. I was conscious that he fastened the door and then came round to the side of the bed where I was lying. He removed the bed-clothes, raised up my nightshirt, and remained for some minutes contemplating me. Of course, the principal object of his worship was my virile member which, as was usual at that period of my life, always held up its head proudly erect when I awoke in the morning. I heard him undress himself and get into bed, and then kneeling down by my side, after kissing and caressing my organ of pleasure, he took the point of it into his mouth and commenced sucking it and moving it backwards and forwards between his lips. I opened my eyes, as if just awakened, and beheld him kneeling beside me perfectly naked with his tremendous member standing stiff and erect. He immediately made me take off my shirt, and employed himself for a time in examining me all over and caressing all my charms. During this time I also made a more minute inspection of my acquaintance of the preceding evening, and I was even more than ever astonished at its proportions, and at how I had managed ever to get it within my narrow aperture as far as it had been.

After some little time had elapsed in these preliminaries, he said that it was his turn now to contribute to my enjoyment, and taking hold of my weapon, he was going to turn himself away from where Laura and Frank were placed. As they had both been greatly interested by the account I had given them of Sir Charles' tremendous weapon, I wished that they should have an opportunity of seeing as much as possible of its proceedings. So I got him to change his position and to place himself where they were and where they could have the gratification of observing every motion he made in the approaching encounter. He immediately placed himself as I wished, and I then, at his request, took up my position behind him, and he proceeded to introduce my weapon into the sheath of pleasure. But if I had been surprised at the largeness of one of his proportions, I was no less so at the smallness of the other, as in fact I had almost as much difficulty in getting into him as he had had with me. At length, with his assistance, I succeeded and gradually penetrated within the delightful cavity, till I was completely imbedded within it. Of course, the opposition I met with and the extreme tightness of the place, when it was once fairly overcome, only increased the pleasurable sensations I experienced after I had fairly accomplished my entrance. When he found I was completely buried within him and was beginning to proceed with the work of pleasure, he took my hand and placed it on his majestic champion, saying that if I would be good enough to operate upon it at the same time it would not only give him exquisite pleasure by being combined with the performance going on behind, but would also, by depriving it of a little of its vehement fury, make our after-proceedings more easy and agreeable to me, when, as he hoped I would allow him to do, he should again try to introduce it into the delicious aperture that had given him so much delight the previous day. I immediately acquiesced, and grasping as much of the pillar as I could manage to do with one hand, I commenced a series of movements upon it, gently rubbing it up and down and titillating the shaft as much as possible, which drew from him the warmest encomiums. In this manner, combining the movements of my hand in front with those of my excited weapon in the rear, I managed to pour my tribute into him at the same time that he sent a shower of love's balsam spouting beyond the bed far into the room.

This scene acted so powerfully on Laura that unable to restrain herself, as Frank afterwards told me, she seized hold of his hand, conveyed it to her pleasure-spot, and made him cool her raging fever in a similar manner where she stood.

Sir Charles then asked if I would allow him to endeavour to accomplish the undertaking which it had given him so much delight partially to accomplish the preceding day. I could not well make any objection, after having availed myself of his complaisance, to his now proceeding to carry out his wishes to their entire fulfilment. I therefore disposed myself so as to endeavour to stand the attacks in as favourable a position as I could, and at the same time afforded my friends as good a view of the proceedings as was possible.

I placed all the pillows and cushions I could find on a heap in the centre of the bed and lay down with my belly resting on them so as to raise up my posteriors and present them to him in an attitude that would be propitious to his purpose. He thanked me, and told me to let him know if I found that he hurt me too much and he would at once stop, as he would be sorry to enjoy even such a gratification if it were to be at the expense of occasioning me any suffering. He had provided some ointment with which he lubricated the whole of his weapon, and then with his finger inserted some of it in my aperture. He then applied the point of the dart to the mark, and endeavoured to insert it. For some time it baffled his endeavours, the head slipping upwards and downwards, away from the entrance, whenever he attempted to thrust which he did very gently and carefully. I saw he was too much afraid of hurting me to be able to succeed, and getting excited myself by this time, put my hand between my thighs and taking hold of his splendid weapon I kept its head at the mouth of the aperture, and desired him to thrust a little more boldly. At the same time, trying to push back and stretch the aperture as much as possible, I met his advancing thrusts with all the firmness I could muster. This brought about the junction I desired, and again to his great delight the head of his weapon got lodged between the extended lips of the aperture. The pain, however, of this proceeding was so great that I was obliged to ask him to pause till it should abate a little, which it very soon did. Then summoning up courage, I told him to thrust again gently. This he hastened to do in the most delicate manner possible. The first few thrusts, till the upper part of the pillar got fairly inserted within the cheeks, were even worse than before. But as soon as this was accomplished, and the hollow part at the junction of the pillar with the head passed the Rubicon, all feeling of uneasiness vanished and was succeeded by the most delicious sensations, as inch by inch he gradually fought his way into my interior, the intense pleasure increasing at every thrust he gave, until the whole of the monster was fairly established within me, and I could feel the hair on his thighs and belly in close contact with my buttocks, and his delightful soft bullets beat against mine at every motion he made. As soon as he was fully lodged to the utmost extent within the citadel, he stopped and inquired how I felt and expressed the greatest satisfaction at finding my sufferings had now been converted into pleasure. After enjoying the voluptuous sensations of the elastic constriction the nerves of the sheath in which it was plunged exerted upon his throbbing weapon for some minutes, during which his hands roved over my body in nervous agitation, he resumed his delightful exercise, and thrust after thrust of his delicious weapon was driven into me with the most intense enjoyment to both parties. At length, his lusty efforts were rewarded with success, and, from the warm gush within me, I felt that a torrent of bliss must have issued from him, while his nervous frame shook and quivered with blissful agitation and enjoyment as the extasy of delight came over him. He lay for a few minutes bathed in enjoyment, and then raising his head, thanked me most fervently for all the bliss I had conferred on him and expressed his hope that it had been accomplished without much suffering on my part. In answer I gently turned both him and myself on one side, too much delighted with its presence to allow his sword to escape from my scabbard, and made him look at the pillow on which my weapon had rested, and where a plenteous effusion of the balmy liquid plainly attested that I too had shared in the delights of his enjoyment. He expressed his great gratification at this, as he said the sole drawback to his enjoyment had been the fear that it had been attained at my expense. But he said that what he now saw

73

emboldened him to make a new request, and as the difficulty had now been overcome, to ask whether I might be persuaded to allow him still to retain his present quarter and enjoy another victory. I readily agreed. I told him that the sensations produced upon me by the insertion of his weapon in so sensitive a place was so agreeable – that it was so was, indeed, very evident from the powerful manner in which it still affected mine – that he must allow it to remain quietly where it was for a time and let me enjoy the agreeable sensation of its presence there.

He said he could desire nothing better, and we lay for a considerable period thus pleasantly conjoined. During this time I purposely turned the conversation upon Laura and Frank. I began by joking him about what Laura would say if she saw us in such a situation defrauding her of her just rights. He replied that he did not know what she would say, but that he knew what she ought to say, or at least what he would say if he were to find her in a similar situation, and that was that as she could not assist in contributing to his happiness at present, she was very glad to find that he had been able to get somebody else who could.

'Then,' said I, 'you would not be offended, if she were to follow your example.'

'No, certainly not,' was his reply. 'I don't mean to say that I would not rather prefer that I should have her entirely to myself, but I am so fond of her that if I found it would contribute to her happiness to enjoy herself with another, I should not make the slightest objection, provided she would only allow me to contribute to her enjoyment as much as I could.' He went on to say that he was sadly afraid she would never allow him that pleasure, that he did once hope she might have been induced to accept him, but for the last few weeks, with the exception of the previous night, she had been colder than ever, and he was afraid to press her on the subject for fear of being at once rejected.

I ventured cautiously to express my opinion that he was too

distrustful of his own merits, and that he stood higher in Laura's favour than he seemed to imagine.

He eagerly caught at my words, and asked on what grounds I thought so. He said he saw that from my old acquaintance with her as a boy, I was on more intimate terms with her than anyone else and more likely to understand her sentiments, and that he had often thought of speaking to me on the subject. Indeed, he said he would almost have been jealous of my influence with her had I been a few years older and had it not been that, instead of appearing to be annoyed at his attentions to her, I had rather given him every opportunity to pursue them.

As I felt he was watching me, I endeavoured to keep my countenance as well as I could, but I was aware that the blood mounting in my cheeks must to some extent betray the secret interest I took in the subject. I thought the best plan was to acknowledge that from our early intimacy, and the kindness she had always shown me, I did take a great interest in her, and that it was perhaps only my being sensible that she could neither look up to nor respect one so much younger than herself that prevented this feeling from ripening into a warmer attachment, but that I was old enough to be able to wish to promote her happiness even if I could not myself be the means of doing so, and that from what I had seen of her feelings towards him, I had always thought they might be happy together, and consequently had wished him success.

He pressed me very much regarding what she thought, or might have said of him.

I told him that of course it was not a subject on which I could have ventured to speak to her seriously, that sometimes a looker-on saw more of the game than the players, and that I thought she did like him and was only restrained from showing it more by his not urging his suit so much as he perhaps might have done. We had some further conversation on the subject, and I added that I knew she was of a reserved disposition as regarded her own feelings and did not like to have them noticed and commented on by strangers and that perhaps the idea of all the parade and show which he might think necessary at the celebration of his marriage and the discussion of the matter for months previously might annoy her, while she would probably have been more easily induced to consent had he been a person of less rank and consequence, when all this exhibition would have been avoided.

He said that if she had any difficulty on this ground, nothing could be easier than to obviate it, for as far as he was concerned it would give him the greatest satisfaction to dispense with all formalities, except necessary settlements which he would take care should not occupy much time, and they might be quietly married at their own church in the neighbourhood without making any fuss about it; that with the exception of his mother and sister he had no relations he cared anything about or whom he would wish to be present, so that Laura could have everything her own way.

Without attempting to urge too much, I gave him to understand that I thought he had better come to an explanation with her as soon as possible and make her aware of his ideas on these points. And I promised to endeavour to ascertain her wishes as far as I could and make him acquainted with them.

I had long felt by the unruliness of his member, which was deeply imbedded within me, how powerful an impression the discussion of this subject produced upon him. He very soon disregarded my injunctions to keep quiet – the delightful intruder would keep wandering up and down in the path of pleasure – and before our conversation was concluded, I felt the warm injection twice spouted into me. After this, he said he would not venture to trespass upon my kindness any further for the present, and urged me to take his place, which, excited as I was by his performances, I was very well disposed to do. He made every arrangement for my entering him in the most agreeable manner, inserting the weapon himself and tickling and playing with the appendages.

When fairly entered and enjoying myself to the utmost, I laughingly said that if he was going to run away with Laura I could not hope for any long continuance of our present agreeable amusement and I must try if I could persuade Frank to allow me to enjoy with him some of the pleasant pastimes he had been teaching me. He eagerly caught at the idea and urged me to do so, offering to leave with me all his books and pictures to show to him, and telling me to let him have any of them he liked, and at the same time begging me, if I succeeded, to allow him to join in our amusements, as the possession of one resembling Laura so much would be the next thing to enjoying herself. This was exactly what I wanted, for I felt satisfied that after having enjoyed the brother he could never complain of anything the sister might do. Having then brought my enterprise to a satisfactory termination, I made him leave me, and joined Laura and Frank.

Although they had been able to see everything, they had not heard all that passed. Coming to my bed, they proceeded to satisfy the burning desires which the scene they had just witnessed had lighted up in them. While thus agreeably employed, I joked Laura about the martyrdom I had undergone for her sake and what she was to look forward to suffer when she attempted to take in the stupendous instrument whose performances she had just seen. She did not appear to be much afraid of it, and said that judging from the manner in which I had apparently enjoyed its presence within me there was not much reason for apprehension. But she eagerly asked what we had been talking about, as she had heard only so far as to make out that she was the subject of our discourse. She was quite delighted to find that the result had been so satisfactory, and it was at once resolved that, when Sir Charles pressed the matter, she would consent and that I should contrive to impress upon him the propriety of his urging the completion of the marriage and as little delay and ceremony as possible.

Frank and I made up a party to ride with them that forenoon, and we took care to let them have an opportunity for an explanation. Laura was in a gracious mood. Sir Charles acted on my advice, pressed his suit, was accepted, explained his own wish to have the marriage concluded as soon as possible, but at the same time saying that on that point as on every other he should wish to consult her feelings in every respect, and was given to understand that her sentiments coincided with his. Having obtained her consent, he spoke to her father as soon as we returned from our ride, and as the settlements he proposed were most satisfactory, it was at once arranged. And it was settled that the marriage should take place within a month.

When Sir Charles came to me the next morning, he was in extasies at the successful termination of his suit, which he asserted was in a great measure due to my good advice, and he urged me to attend him on the happy occasion. As this afforded a good excuse for my remaining at the Hall, and being on a good footing with Laura, I readily agreed. Laura having expressed a wish that they should be quiet during the few weeks she was to remain at home, it was arranged that the visits of some friends who were expected should be postponed. Her aunt, immediately on hearing of the marriage, returned to the Hall, but I made Laura give her mother a hint that, though she did not like to say so to her aunt herself, she would prefer being allowed to enjoy the privacy of an apartment by herself. Her mother thought this was quite reasonable, and another room was prepared for Miss Middleton. Frank was allowed to remain at home till after the marriage, and we thus secured another month of our delightful pastime to which we gave ourselves up without scruple or reserve. Sir Charles, though unwilling to tear himself away from the pleasure he was enjoying and anticipating, was obliged to go to town to make the necessary arrangements. I was desirous before he went to take a photographic view of him in the act of enjoying me, as I thought that in the event of Laura being obliged to have recourse to any compulsion upon him, her object would be better attained by making him aware she was in possession of such a picture than by any reference to me or explanation as to how she came to know anything on the subject. It was necessary for this purpose to bring Frank on the scene. As he was quite willing to join in the sport, having been greatly taken with what he had witnessed of Sir Charles' operations, I told the latter that by means of his pictures I had come to a good understanding with him and that he had agreed to comply with our wishes. Giving him to believe that there was a double maidenhead to be taken, I proposed that they should both be disposed of at the same time, and offered him his choice which he would prefer. He said that if it was left to him to decide he would prefer to make the attack in the rear, and we settled that he should come to me the next morning when I could get Frank to meet us.

Frank was in bed with me when Sir Charles arrived. I at once turned down the bed-clothes stripped off his shirt and exhibited him quite naked, his fiery little dart, standing erect and unhooded, exhibiting its proportions in the most splendid manner, and I asked if he had ever seen anything more beautiful. He threw himself on the charming boy and covered every part of him with kisses, while I undressed him and reduced him to a similar state of nakedness as ourselves. As soon as this was done, I prepared Frank for the sacrifice. I was apprehensive that there would be as much difficulty in introducing the magnificent weapon into his lovely, but narrow aperture as there had been in my own case, and I endeavoured to provide against the worst as satisfactorily as I could. I knelt down on the bed and made him place himself kneeling also so as to rest his belly on my back. Sir Charles then placed himself behind him and grasped him firmly round the loins, making his splendid weapon appear between his thighs, where I saw it rubbing fiercely against Frank's less mature organ. Taking hold of it and making it move back a little, I introduced my hand between Frank's thighs, and separating the lips of the delicious aperture between his lovely buttocks, I directed the point of the throbbing monster to the proper spot. Holding it firmly in the requisite position, I told Sir Charles to press it gently forwards. This he immediately did and to my great astonishment I felt it gradually advancing and slipping into the gulf of pleasure without difficulty, till I was obliged to withdraw the grasp my hand held on it. I had hardly done so when I saw the enormous pillar entirely swallowed up, and on turning my eyes to Frank's face, I could not discover on his countenance the slightest trace of pain or suffering. Satisfied that I need have no further apprehension on his account, I turned myself a little round, so as to take my part in the play, and placing myself directly before him, so as to bring my buttocks in contact with his warm soft belly, I insinuated Frank's charming little darling into my rear. While holding me fast with one arm round the middle, he grasped my stiffly erected standard with the other hand. Thinking that the power and weight of metal of Sir Charles' performer in the rear would prevent Frank from exerting himself much in the combat, I resolved to render any great exertion on his part unnecessary. For keeping time with Sir Charles' motions, I commenced a series of heaves by which, whenever Sir Charles' weapon was fully driven up to the hilt in his hinder quarter, his own was as fully and as pleasantly introduced within me. This delightful operation very soon produced such a state of extatic delirium that he could not refrain from giving vent to the most enthusiastic praises of our performances in such a loud tone that I was obliged to beg him to be quiet to prevent suspicion being aroused. The delight was too excessive to endure long, and before Sir Charles was ready to perform his part in the final scene, I felt dear Frank's discharge poured into me, as his head sank upon my back and his convulsive grasp of my throbbing instrument relaxed. I retained him in this position for a few seconds longer, while the fierce heaves of Sir Charles, driving his steed to and fro in the delicious field of battle, testified to the soul-stirring effect that had been produced upon him and soon relieved his high mettled charger of a portion of his superabundant fluid. Then withdrawing from Frank, he laid him down on the bed, and again renewed his caresses which very soon reanimated the slightly drooping head of his darling charmer.

We agreed, however, that it would be better to allow Frank to be passive in the next encounter, and accordingly I took the centre position, and entering Frank's delicious rear, I exposed my own to be breached by the enormous battering ram of Sir Charles. The assault, however, was not nearly so terrible, and with a little care I now contrived to take it all in, and speedily enjoyed the felicity of feeling its throbbing pulsation beating within me over the whole extent of the cavity which it so completely filled up. Frank's charming receptacle for my own heaving instrument was of that pleasing elasticity that I should not have discovered it had ever once been invaded by a larger weapon than my own, and the voluptuous sensations it produced upon my burning member as, excited to the highest pitch and swollen to the utmost extension, the fiery dart was plunged in and out of the burning furnace, were most exquisite. I felt, too, the full effect which Frank had already experienced of the greatly increased pleasure during the amorous encounter which resulted from the pressure in the interior of so large an instrument as that of Sir Charles. And much as I had enjoyed my former encounters with them both separately, most assuredly this one, in which they both combined their utmost efforts to produce the most lascivious sensations it is possible to conceive, far surpassed everything that had taken place previously.

Another scene of delicious toying succeeded. The darling objects which had already given us so much delight were again investigated and admired, and each new proof of the bliss they were capable of conferring upon us only made us more eager to offer up our worship to them. Another delicious combat succeeded. Sir Charles this time took the combat-position, and I again received his member within me. But my concern being now well saturated with the blissful libations that had been already poured into it, the monster slipped into me this time with very little difficulty. Frank, on the other hand, was delighted as well as surprised to discover that he had no easy task to force his way into the agreeable fortress he was about to storm in Sir Charles' rear. But the difficulty only enhanced the pleasure when the breach was fairly made, and the invader revelled in full and undisputed possession of the interior works. And if I might judge from the exclamations of delight, they both enjoyed themselves to their hearts' content when they had once gained admission to their respective destinations. So much so that after they had run one course they gave no signs of wishing to change their positions. I put my hand behind to ascertain the state of matters, and found both the heroes still in such an excited condition that I said if they were disposed to break another lance in the same lists I was quite willing to keep my place, provided Sir Charles would take my charger in hand and lead him on to participate in the pleasing conflict. This proposal was highly approved of and at once carried into effect, to the entire satisfaction of all parties. After this I made Sir Charles leave us, not wishing that we should be entirely worked out as I was quite aware poor Laura would be in a sad state if she found that we were unable to do anything in the way of appeasing her longings after the excitement she must have undergone while witnessing our voluptuous proceedings.

As soon as he was gone, Laura made her appearance and scolded us heartily for having wasted so much of our precious strength and enjoyed ourselves so completely without her. But as we each contrived to give her pretty satisfactory proof that we had not spent all our treasures, we soon put her in a good humour again; especially as Sir Charles was to leave on the next day, when she would have us all to herself again.

In the course of the day, I easily persuaded Sir Charles to allow me to take likenesses of us all three in the various attitudes of enjoying each other, one of which I took care should be sealed up and deposited where Laura would have it at command in the event of her finding it necessary to have recourse of it, even if I should not be at hand at the time. As Sir Charles was obliged after this to be almost constantly absent, we gave up to him the few nights he occasionally spent at the Hall, and the remainder were passed with Laura in a constant series of repetitions of delightful sports which, however agreeable to the actors, would involve a tiresome repetition were I to detail them.

The only variety was Frank's adventure with Betsy. Having been once accustomed to indulge his passions, he regretted sadly that the enjoyment would continue only for so short a period, as Laura and her Charles were to go abroad immediately on their marriage, and he began to look about him for some object to console him in her absence. He soon fixed upon Betsy, but he found it more difficult to obtain her consent than he had expected. When I joked her on the subject, she admitted that she liked the boy, but said she was afraid there was a great risk that he might talk of it and get her into a scrape. Finding that Frank was very desirous to have her, I agreed to promote his wishes. I had endeavoured to conceal as much as possible from Betsy my intercourse with Laura, but she was too quick not to have discovered that there existed a good understanding between us, though I still pretended that although we were sometimes in the habit of amusing ourselves together after her old fashion she had not yet granted me the last favour. I now told her that Laura had discovered my intercourse with her, and that previous to her own marriage she wished to see us perform the conjugal rites that she might know how to conduct herself when it came to be her turn, and that I had therefore arranged, as Frank was to be out early the next morning, Laura was to come to my room where I had promised that Betsy and I should comply with her wishes. Frank got one of his sister's caps which concealed his hair, and a nightshirt which closed in front over his breast, and it was hardly possible for anyone to tell that it was not Laura herself. Indeed, the disguise was so complete that the next time Sir Charles came to enjoy himself with us, I made Frank dress up in the same manner and pretend to be asleep in bed with me, and it was only when I could not restrain a burst of laughter at his consternation that Sir Charles discovered the trick we had played on him. Nor do I think he was perfectly satisfied until the removal of Frank's shirt showed standing proof that it did not cover a woman's form.

Betsy's discovery was made in a different manner. When she came, Frank kept under the bedclothes until I had stripped her, and getting into bed with her performed the hymenial rites in due order. When we had finished, I slipped off her on the other side of the bed from Frank, leaving her lying on her back all exposed to his observation. He commenced a survey of every part of her, joking her on the beauties he discovered and on the manner in which she had enjoyed the operation that had just been performed, and wondering whether it would give her as much satisfaction. Gradually he began to embrace her, and at last got upon her, asking me if that was the way Sir Charles would do it to her.

'Yes that is it,' said I, as he got between her thighs and placed himself in the position in which I had lately been, 'only he would not have this stupid night dress about him, and he will have something stiff between his legs to put into that pretty little hole you see before you, now try what you can do to imitate him.'

While Frank clasped her in his arms and pressed his mouth to hers, I raised his shirt, and pointing his weapon at the mark, he thrust himself forward, and it slipped into her in an instant. Betsy's consternation was extreme as she felt the warm flesh within her. She had on many occasions tried the effect of Laura's substitute, but her experience of the real article had been quite enough to satisfy her that this was something of a different description, and she exclaimed, 'Goodness gracious Miss Laura, what is the meaning of this?'

Frank replied, tearing off his cap and exhibiting his short curls instead of Laura's flowing ringlets, 'Well, I am glad I have got something to prove I am not a girl, for I was beginning to be afraid that the change of dress had effected a complete transformation.'

It was too late for any objection now. Nor did Betsy appear at all disposed to make any. On the contrary, the lascivious boy's motions were so lively and so well directed and his capacity for conferring pleasure so much greater than she had expected that she at once yielded herself up to the enjoyment, and joined in his amorous transports with hearty good will. And when he had given and drawn from her the first proof of their mutual satisfaction with each other and the young rogue still retained his position and proceeded to give her a second dose of his prolific balm, she was quite transported with delight and exerted herself with so much vigour and set to second his endeavours that they very soon sank exhausted in each other's arms enjoying to the utmost the second proof of the completion of their mutual overwhelming bliss.

But these hours of happiness were too delightful to last long. The day appointed for the marriage came upon us before we could believe it possible. Though sorely against my will I thought it right to suggest to Laura whether it would not be prudent that she should pass the last night of her presumed virgin state without having her inmost recesses explored for fear of any traces being left. But though she at first agreed that this precaution would be advisable, she could not make up her mind to put it in practice. To our surprise and joy she came to us as usual as soon as she was left alone for the night. Unwilling to run the risk of her appearing fatigued and exhausted in the morning, we resolved to concentrate our forces upon her and take our farewell that

85

night. Time after time we kept up the amorous combat, sometimes in succession and sometimes combining our forces for a joint attack both in front and rear, almost without intermission until we were fairly exhausted; and it was only when after repeated engagements even her fond caresses failed to revive our enervated champions that, taking an affectionate farewell, she retired to her own apartment. The exercise so far from injuring seemed to have a beneficial effect on her charms, and never had she looked more lovely than she appeared the next morning when she was transferred to the arms of the enraptured Sir Charles.

Most fortunately everything turned out eventually even more agreeably than we had ventured to hope. A few days afterwards I had the gratification of hearing from Laura that she had satisfactorily put in operation the device I had suggested, which, combined with the difficulty Sir Charles experienced from his great size in obtaining an entrance and the pain she pretended to experience when he forced his way within her supposed virgin sanctuary, completely prevented any suspicion on his part. And loving her as I did, I was pleased with her frank avowal that not only his general conduct and kindness left her nothing to wish for, but that in her nuptial intercourse with him she derived if possible even greater pleasure than she enjoyed with us. The symptoms which had alarmed us passed off without producing the dreaded consequence, and it was not till some weeks after the usual time had elapsed that she presented the delighted Sir Charles with a son who was soon followed by numerous successors.

Frank before long joined the army, and in the arms of others soon found consolation, though he never forgot the charms of his first instructress. When Laura and I met again, we could not refrain from renewing our old delights and comparing the changes which had taken place in each other's charms, but with the exception of one single occasion, I believe I am the only one she ever allowed to participate with her husband in the pleasures she was so well calculated to confer.

After the marriage I got alarmed about Betsy, and regretted that I had allowed her to know so much as she did. The only remedy I could devise was to persuade her to go to a distant country where she would have no temptation to speak on the subject. On sounding her, I found that, trusting to the influence she thought she had obtained over Frank and me, she was not disposed to be removed from us. I therefore had recourse to John and found him not only much more intelligent but also more sensible than his mistress. I had not much difficulty in convincing him that if he had the means of settling in Australia he was much more likely to prosper there than by continuing in service in this country.

As a further inducement, and a reason why I took an interest in them, I told him I had discovered that Frank had taken a fancy for Betsy and that, though there was no reason to suppose anything occurred, it would be better they should be separated. He was quite of the same opinion, and as the consequences of the operations of some one of us upon Betsy threatened in a short time to become apparent, he made it a condition of their marriage that she should emigrate with him. As I had a strong suspicion that I had at least dug out the foundation, if not laid the cornerstone, of the structure which Betsy was about to rear, I took care they should have the means to settle comfortably, and from his knowledge in horse breeding, John soon prospered there. Very soon after their arrival in the colony and precisely at the expiration of the usual period from my first entrance within her, she presented her husband with a son. She never had another child.

The
New Epicurean

on

THE DELIGHTS OF SEX

facetiously and

PHILOSOPHICALLY CONSIDERED

in

GRAPHIC LETTERS
addressed to young ladies of quality.

Domi maneas paresque nobis
Novem continuas fututiones.

CATULLUS CARMEN XXXIL

The New Epicurean

Gentle Reader,

Before transcribing my correspondence with my fair friends, it is necessary to describe the scene of the amours alluded to in the letters, and also to say a few words regarding the chief actor, myself.

I am a man who, having passed the Rubicon of youth, has arrived at that age when the passions require a more stimulating diet than is to be found in the arms of every painted courtezan.

That I might the better carry out my philosophical design of pleasure without riot and refined voluptuous enjoyment without alloy, and with safety, I became the purchaser of a suburban villa situated in extensive grounds, embosomed in lofty trees, and surrounded with high walls. This villa I altered to suit my taste and had it so contrived that all the windows faced towards the road, except the French ones, which opened on the lawn from a charming room, to which I had ingress from the grounds at the back and which was quite cut off from the rest of the house. To render these grounds more private, high walls extended like wings from either side of the house and joined the outer walls. I thus secured an area of some five acres of woodland which was not overlooked from any quarter, and where everything that took place would be a secret unknown to the servants in the villa.

The grounds I had laid out in the true English style, with umbrageous walks, alcoves, grottoes, fountains, and every adjunct that could add to their rustic beauty. In the open space, facing the secret apartment before alluded to, was spread out a fine lawn, embossed with beds of the choicest flowers, and in the centre, from a bouquet of maiden's blush roses, appeared a statue of Venus; in white marble at the end of every shady valley was a terminal figure of the god of gardens in his various forms, either bearded like the antique head of the Indian Bacchus, or soft and feminine, as we see the lovely Antinous, or Hermaphroditic – the form of a lovely girl with puerile attributes. In the fountains swam gold and silver fish, whilst rare crystals and spars glittered amidst mother o' pearl at the bottom of the basins.

The gardeners who kept this happy valley in order were only admitted on Mondays and Tuesdays, which days were devoted by me entirely to study, the remaining four being sacred to Venus and love.

This garden had three massive doors in its walls, each fitted with a small lock made for the purpose, and all opened with a gold key which never left my watch guard.

Such were the external arrangements of my Caproe. Now, with a few words on the internal economy of my private *salle d'amour*, and I have done.

This apartment, which was large and lofty, was in its fittings and furniture entirely in Louis Quinze, that is to say, in the latest French mode; the walls were panelled and painted in pale French grey, white and gold, and were rendered less formal by being hung with exquisite paintings by Watteau. Cabinets of buhl and marqueterie lined the sides, each filled with erotic works by the best authors, illustrated with exquisite and exciting prints and charmingly bound. The couches and chairs were of ormolu, covered *en suite* with grey satin, and stuffed with down. The legs of the tables were also gilt, the tops were slabs of marble, which, when not in use for the delicious collations (which were from time to time served up through a trap door in the floor) were covered with rich tapestries. The window curtains were of grey silk and Venetian blinds, painted a pale rose colour, cast a voluptuous shade over the room.

The chimney piece was of marble, large, lofty, and covered with sculpture in relief, representing beautiful naked children of both sexes in every wanton attitude, entwined with grapes and flowers, carved by the hand of a master. The sides and hearth of this elegant fireplace were encrusted with porcelain tiles of rare beauty, representing the Triumph of Venus, and silver dogs were placed on either side to support the wood, according to the style in vogue in the middle of the last century.

To complete the *coup d'œil*, my embroidered suit of garnet velvet, plumed hat, and diamond hilted sword were carelessly flung upon a chair, while the cabinets and sideboards were covered with costly snuff boxes and china. Such were some of the striking features of this delightful chamber. As for the rest of the house, it was furnished like any other respectable domicile of our times.

My establishment consisted of a discreet old house-keeper, who was well paid and not too sharply looked after in the little matters of perquisites and peculations, a bouncing blooming cook, and a sprightly trim housemaid, who were kept in good humour by an occasional half guinea, a holiday, and a chuck under the chin. Beyond these innocent liberties they were not molested. As for the gardeners, they lived out of the house, and being as well paid for their two days' work as if they worked all the week, it followed that they knew their own interests too well to manifest any undue or indiscreet curiosity as to what passed in the grounds when their services were not required.

Having thus given a sketch of the premises, I proceed at once with the letters, only expressing a hope that you, most courteous reader, will quietly lay down the book if it is too strong for your stomach instead of falling foul of

Your humble servant
THE AUTHOR.

To Lesbia

You ask me, most charming Lesbia, to relieve the ennui which your too venerable and too watchful lord causes you to suffer, with his officious attentions, by a recital of some of those scenes which are not visible to the uninitiated; and I, having always been your slave, hasten to obey.

You must know then, *chère petite*, that I have certain convenient ladies in my pay, whom I call pointers, forasmuch as they put up the game.

Last Thursday as I lay stretched on a sofa absorbed in that most charming of Diderot's works *La Religieuse*, the silver bell which communicates with the southern gate gave tongue and roused me from my lethargy. I sprang to my feet and wending my way through that avenue of chestnut trees, which you and I, Lesbia, know so well, made direct for the gate. Here the well-known chariot met my eye, and it only required a glance at the smart coachman to show me that jehu was none other than Madame R. herself; and a devilish handsome groom she made, I can assure you.

An almost imperceptible raising of the eyebrows and a gesture with her whip handle towards the interior of the carriage told me all I wanted to know; so first looking up and down the road to see that we were not observed, I whispered, 'ten o'clock' and then opened the door. 'Come my little darlings,' said I to two young creatures, who, coquettishly dressed with the most charming little hats in the world and full petticoats that barely reached their rose coloured garters, sprang, nothing loth, into my arms. The next minute we were all three standing in the garden, the door was locked, and the chariot drove off. The elder of my little pets was a blooming blonde, with soft brown hair that shone like gold, melting eyes of the loveliest blue, and cheeks tinted with the softest blush of the rose, a pert little nose slightly retroussé, carmine lips, and teeth like pearls completed a most delicious face. She was, she said, just seventeen years old. Her companion, a sparkling brunette with dark eyes, raven hair, and a colour that vied with the damask rose, was about sixteen. They were charming girls, and when I tell you that their limbs were moulded in the most perfect symmetry and that their manners were cultivated, elegant, and gay, I think you will agree with me that Madame R. had catered well.

'Now my little loves,' said I, giving each a kiss, 'what shall we do first; are you hungry, will you eat?'

This proposal seemed to give great satisfaction, so taking each by the hand I led them to my room; and patties, strawberries and cream, apricots, and champagne disappeared with incredible rapidity. While they were eating, I was exploring; now patting the firm dimpled peach-like bottom of the pretty brunette, now inserting a finger into the pouting hairless cleft of the lovely blonde. The latter was called Blanche and the former Cerise. I was beside myself with rapture, and turning first to one and then to the other, covered them with kisses. The collation finished at last, we all went into the grounds, and having walked them round and shown them everything curious, not forgetting the statue of that most impudent god Priapus, at whose grotesque appearance, with his great prick sticking out, they laughed heartily, I proposed to give them a swing. Of course in putting them in I took care that their lovely little posteriors should bulge out beyond the velvet seat, and as their clothes were short, every time they swung high in the air I had a full expansive view of those white globes, and the tempting rose coloured slits that pouted between them; then, oh! the dear little feet, the fucktious shoes, the racy delectable legs; nothing could be finer. But the sight was too tantalising. We were all heated; I with the exertion of swinging them, they with the wine, so they readily agreed to my proposal to proceed to a retired spot, where was a little lake lined with marble not more than four feet deep. We were soon naked and sporting in the water; then only was it that I could take in all their loveliness at a glance. The small pointed breasts; the polished ivory shoulders, the exquisite fall in the back, the tiny waist, the bulging voluptuous hips, the dimpled bottoms, blushing and fresh, the plump thighs and smooth white bellies. In a moment my truncheon stood up hard and firm as a constable's staff. I put it in their hands, I frigged and kissed their fragrant cunnies, I gamahuched them, and then the saucy Cerise, taking my ruby tipped ferrule in her little rosy mouth, began rolling her tongue round it in such a way that I nearly fainted with bliss. At that moment our position was this: I lay stretched on my back on the grass; Blanche sat over me, a leg on either side, with my tongue glued to her rose. Cerise knelt astride of me also, with her posteriors well jutted out towards me, and one of my fingers was inserted in her rosebud. Nor were the hands of the delicious brunette idle; with her right she played with my balls and with the forefinger of her left hand she exquisitely titillated the regions beneath. But human nature could not stand this long; so changing our position I placed Blanche on her hands and knees while Cerise inserted my arrow, covered with saliva from her mouth, into the pretty Blanche. She was tight, but not a virgin, so after a thrust or two I fairly went in up to the hilt. All this while Cerise was tickling me and rubbing her beautiful body against me. Soon Blanche began to spend, and to sigh out, 'Oh! oh! dear sir, give it me now! Shoot it into me! Ah I faint! I die!' and as the warm fluid gushed into her she fell prone on the ground.

When Blanche had a little recovered herself we again plunged into the lake to wash off the dew of love with which we were drenched.

Thus sporting in the water, toying with each other, we whiled away the hours of the afternoon, till tired, at length, we left the lake and dressed ourselves. The sun had long disappeared behind the trees and the shades of evening began to close in. I therefore proposed to adjourn to the villa, where for some time I amused my little friends with bawdy books and prints. But you are not to suppose that my hands were idle, one being under the clothes of each.

Cerise had thrust her hand into my breeches and was manipulating with great industry, which amused me very much; but I soon found out the reason, for presently she said, pouting out her pretty mouth, 'You like Blanche better than me!'

'I love you both, my angels,' said I, laughing heartily at the little puss's jealousy.

'Ah, it's all very well to laugh,' cried Cerise, 'but I don't see why I am not to be fucked as well as her!'

'Oh!' I exclaimed, 'that's the way the wind blows, is it!' And drawing the sweet girl to a couch I tossed up her clothes in a moment.

'Quick, quick, Blanche!' cried Cerise, 'come and gamahuche the gentleman and make his yard measure stiff before he begins, for you know how tight I am at first.'

The little Blanche flung down the book she was looking at, and running up to me placed herself on her knees; then clasping my naked thighs with her milky arms she seized upon the red head of my thyrsus and worked her mouth up and down upon it in the most luscious manner possible. In a few minutes more I could certainly have spent on her tongue had not Cerise, fearful of being baulked, made her leave off. Then guiding the randy prick into her opening rosy little cunny, she began to bound and wriggle and twist until she had worked it well in; then twining her legs around my loins and thrusing her tongue in my mouth she gave way unrestrained to the joys of sensation. Blanche I had thought most delicious, but there was a furore in Cerise's fucking which carried you away, as it were, out of yourself.

So great was the delight I experienced with this amorous girl, that I held back as long as possible but she bounded about with such energy that she soon brought down another shower of dew, and all was over. I was glad to hid the diminished head of poor Pego in my white silk breeches, and it being now nearly ten o'clock I rang for chocolate, which soon appeared through the trap door, served up in pretty little porcelain cups with ratafia cakes and bonbons, to which the girls did ample justice. The bell having announced Madame R. at the gate, we went forth hand in hand, having first placed in their pockets a bright new guinea apiece.

Arrived at the gate, I gave her ladyship a pocket book containing twenty pounds, with which she seemed well content.

'Adieu, dear girls,' said I; 'I hope before long you will pay me another visit.'

'Good-bye, sir,' cried both girls in a breath, and the chariot drove off.

Quite tired by this time, I locked the gate, and going round to the front of the villa I knocked and entered, as if I had just come home, retiring soon after to bed to dream over again of the joys of that delightful evening.

To Lais

I am afraid, my pretty Lais, I am in disgrace with you for not writing before, so to excuse my seeming neglect, I will now narrate to you an adventure I have lately had here which will amuse you very much. You may remember, possibly, pretty Mrs H., the wife of an old prig of a grocer, whom you met here once. Well, she came to see me the other day when, after I had done justice to her charms, which indeed are not to be despised, sitting on my knee and sipping some old Burgundy, for which the fine dame has a great liking, she told me the cause of her visit.

'As you are so generous,' she began, 'it always gives me great pleasure to oblige you and throw anything in your way that is worthy of the notice of such a true Epicurean. Now I have just received from the country a niece whose father has been long dead and has now lost her mother, so the good people of the place where they lived, to get rid of the orphan, have sent her up to me. This has vexed my good man not a little, as you know he loves his money dearly; not able to get a child for himself, he has no fancy to be saddled with other people's. But I quieted him with the assurance that I would get her a place in a few days. The girl is nineteen years old, as beautiful and fresh as an angel and innocent as a baby, so I thought what a nice amusement it would be for you to have her here and enlighten and instruct her. You have, I know, a little cottage fitted up as a dairy; engage her as your dairymaid, buy a cow or two, and the thing is done.'

'But,' said I, 'won't she be afraid to live in the cottage all alone, and if the gardeners should find it out what would they think!'

'Nay, sir,' said the tempter, 'your honour knows best, but it seems to me that these difficulties can easily be got over. I know an old crone, a simple, poor, humble creature, who would do anything for half a crown and be delighted to live in that cottage. She alone will be seen by the gardeners, and my niece will be kept close during the two days they work in the grounds.'

'That will do capitally,' said I. 'You arrange it all.' Accordingly, old mother Jukes and the blooming Phoebe were duly installed. Two alderney cows occupied the cowhouse and the new dairymaid set to work. After two or three days had passed, I went one afternoon to see her milk the cows. She jumped up from her three-legged stool in confusion, and blushing deeply, dropped me a rustic curtsey.

'Well, Phoebe,' said I gently, 'what do you think of the dairy? Do you think you shall like the place?'

She dropped me another curtsey, and replied, 'Yes, an't please ye, sir.'

'You find the cottage convenient?' said I.

'Oh! la sir, mighty,' cried Phoebe.

'Very good,' said I, 'now when you have done milking, I will show you the poultry yard and my pet animals, all of which are to be under your care.'

As soon as the fair creature had drawn off as much milk as she required, she placed her pails in the dairy and, smoothing down her white apron, attended me. First to the poultry yard, when Phoebe espied the cock treading one of the hens.

'Oh, my,' she exclaimed, 'that cruel cock; look at him, a pecking, and trampling upon that poor hen, that is just the way they used to go on at feyther's, but I won't let un do it.'

And she ran forward to drive away the cock.

'Stop, stop, Phoebe,' I exclaimed; 'do not drive him away, for if the cock does not tread the hen, how are we to have any chickens?'

'Sure sir, the chickens come from the eggs, and if he treads upon the poor hen that way, he will break them all in her belly, other while.'

'Not at all,' said I. 'It is true pullets lay eggs, and very good are such eggs for eating, but they will never come to chickens. It is the cocks who make the chickens.'

Phoebe opened her large blue eyes very wide at this, and ejaculated, 'Mighty!'

'Don't you see, Phoebe, that while he is treading, he is also doing something else?'

'Noa, sir, I doant,' said Phoebe demurely.

'If you look at the hen's tail, Phoebe, you will see that it is lifted up and spread open; there, now look; and you will see the cock is putting something in the opening under her tail.'

'Oh, la, yes,' cried she, blushing as red as a peony; 'I see now, well I never.'

'You see, Phoebe, you have much to learn; but come to the stable and I will show you something more extraordinary. Where, may I ask, do you suppose foals come from? And kittens, and puppies?'

'Lawk sir, from their mothers, I suppose.'

'Yes, but they would not come without they were made; now you shall see what my little stallion pony will do when I let him into the stall of the mare, and some months hence you shall see the foal he has made.'

To this Phoebe could only respond, 'Mighty.'

We went to the stable. The ponies were beautiful little creatures, of a fine cream colour, and pure Pegu breed, sent to me from Burma by a friend.

Like all horses of that colour, their noses, pizzle, etc., were flesh colour, and therefore at once caught the eye. Removing the bar that divided the loose box, I let the stallion pass into

102

the other side. The little mare received him with a neigh of welcome.

'Oh, my,' cried Phoebe, 'she seems to know him quite nat'ral loike.'

The stallion began nibbling at different parts of the mare, who raised her tail, and again neighed. Her lover answered the neigh. Soon he began to scent her sexual beauties, which he caressed with his lips, his enormous yard shot out and banged against his stifle. I pointed it out to Phoebe.

'Oh, good lud! yes, sir, I see it!' cried she, blushing up very red and trembling all over.

I passed my arm round her taper waist and gently kissing her, whispered, 'Now observe what he will do.'

Presently the stallion mounted on his hind legs, embracing the mare with the fore ones, his great pizzle began to enter; the mare stood firm and did not kick. He laid his head along her back, nibbling her coat. He moved backwards and forwards. Phoebe trembled and turned red and pale by turns. The mare whinnied with delight, the stallion responded.

'See, Phoebe,' said I, 'how these lovers enjoy themselves. Mon Dieu! how happy the are!'

'La sir,' cried the girl, 'what pleasure can there be in having that great long thing put into her body?'

'The pleasure,' said I sententiously, 'which nature gives to those who propagate their kind, and some day my little Phoebe will feel the same pleasure; but look! He has finished, and is out again. See how the female parts of the mare open and shut with spasms of delight. Observe how she cocks her tail – see how she turns her head, as if asking for more. There now, she neighs again.'

But Phoebe was not listening; she had seated herself on a truss of hay, and with her eyes fixed on the again stiffening pizzle of the stallion had fallen into a reverie. I guessed what she was thinking about, so seating myself by her side I stole a hand up her clothes. She trembled, but did not resist. I felt her firm plump thighs, I explored higher, I touched her

103

feather; soft and silky as a mouse's skin was the moss in which I entwined my fingers. I opened the lips, heavens! could I believe my senses. She was spending and her shift was quite wet. Whether it was accident or not I cannot say, but she had dropped one of her hands on my lap.

My truncheon had long been stiff as iron; this additional aggravation had such an effect that, with a start, away flew two material buttons and Jack sprang out of his box into her hand. At this she gave a little scream, and snatching away her own hand at the same time, pushed away mine, and jumping up, began smoothing down her rumpled clothes, and with great vehemence exclaiming,

'Oh, la; fie, sir: doantee, doantee. Oh, I'm afeard,' etc., etc.

But I was not going to lose such a chance and began to soothe her and talk, until at length we got back to the same position again. I grew more bold, I kissed her eyes and her bosom; I handled her lovely buttocks; I frigged her clitoris – her eyes sparkled; she seized upon that weapon which had at first so frightened her, and the next minute I had flung her back on the hay and was frigging away at her maidenhead, but she made a terrible outcry and struggled most violently. Fortunately, Mrs Jukes had a convenient attack of deafness, and heard nothing, so that after a good deal of trouble I found my self in possession of the fortress, up to the hilt. Once in, I knew well how to plant my touches, and ere long a soft languor pervaded all her limbs, pleasure succeeded pain. She no longer repulsed me, but sobbing on my shoulder, stopped now and then to kiss my cheek.

Her climax came at length and then she threw all modesty aside, entwined her lovely legs around my back, twisted, wriggled, bit, pinched, and kissing me with ardour, seemed to wake up to the new life she had found.

Thrice we renewed the seraphic joys; and then and not till then did I leave her to her poultry yard and her dairy.

She is still with me; an adept in the wiles of love; not the least jealous, but very useful to me in all other little affairs which I have on hand. As for Mrs H., I gave her fifty guineas for her niece's maidenhead; and although I have bought many much dearer, I never enjoyed it as I did with Phoebe.

So now good night, and if you can sleep without a lover after such a recital, it is more than I can; so I shall seek the arms of this unsophisticated country lass to allay the fires that recording this narrative has lit up in my veins.

To Sappho

You complain, my sweet girl, that it is long since you heard from me, and remind me that I, of all men, am the only one who could ever give you delight. In reply to your complaint, I must assure you that had there been anything to relate which would have been likely to interest my young philosopher I should have written, but I know too well that ordinary love affairs between men and women do not much amuse you and that the loves of girls for each other are more to your taste. By your other remark I am much flattered; and if you can frame some excuse to your aunt for leaving home and will come here, I think I can show you how to pass an agreeable afternoon. In the interim I will detail an adventure which I met with the other day, and I think will vastly please your fancy.

I was strolling out in one of those thick woods which abound in this neighbourhood when in a secluded dell I espied two young ladies seated very lovingly together, engaged in earnest conversation. They were so absorbed in their discourse that I found no difficulty in approaching softly to within a yard of the spot and, concealing myself in a thicket, sat down on the turf to listen to them.

The elder of the two was a fine handsome woman of about five or six and twenty, with lustrous dark eyes, black hair, an aquiline nose, and noble figure, yet rather too masculine looking to be altogether pleasing. Her companion was a lovely girl of eighteen, a most exquisite face of a perfect oval, laughing blue eyes shaded with long black lashes, and a profusion of the most beautiful hair of a light auburn which wantoned in the breeze in a hundred lovelocks, forming a most charming picture; her figure was exquisitely rounded in all the witchery of early girlhood, and its undulations raised certain strong desires in my heart to be better acquainted with its beauties.

I now set myself to listen to their conversation.

'I assure you,' the dark-eyed woman was saying, 'there is nothing in it; these men are the most selfish creatures in the world; and besides what pleasure, think you, can they give us that we do not have already without their aid?'

'Well, dear friend,' laughed the girl, in a sweet silvery voice, 'I am sure you talk very sensibly, but yet there must be something in the joys of love, if we are to believe the poets, who have so often made it their theme; besides, I do not mind telling you that I know a little more about the subject than you may suppose.'

'Mon Dieu,' ejaculated the dark beauty, who I now began to think was a Frenchwoman, especially as I had already noticed a slight foreign accent in her voice; 'Mon Dieu' (and she turned pale) 'how is it possible you should know anything of love at your age?'

'Shall I tell you?' replied the young girl.

'Ah! yes, yes; tell me, ma chère.'

'Well then dear; you know young Mrs Leslie?'

'Certainly.'

'She was a former school-fellow of mine; and a month or two after her honeymoon, I went on a visit to that pretty country seat of her husband's, Harpsdeen Court, in Bedfordshire. While there she not only told me all about the secret joys of matrimony, but permitted me to witness her bliss.'

'To witness it? Incredible!'

"'Tis a fact, I do assure you; shall I tell you what I saw, and how I saw it?'

'Oh yes, *ma petite*, I do not mind what you may have seen, I was only afraid one of these perfidious men had captivated your poor little heart; as it was a mere girlish frolic, it will amuse me very much to hear all about it.'

The young girl, first giving her friend a sweet kiss, which I envied, thus began:

'My friend Clara Leslie, though not strictly handsome, has a pleasing amiable face, but nature, you know, is full of compensations, as her husband found out to his great satisfaction. She has a shape that vied with the Venus de Medici, the most lovely figure you ever beheld. When quite a girl at school, she could show a leg that any woman might envy, but now at twenty years of age she surpassed the finest statue I ever saw. I will not trouble you with a recapitulation of all that passed on her wedding night, and subsequently up to my arrival at Harpsdeen, because you, my sweet friend, doubtless know all that occurs on such occasions, but will confine myself to what I saw. She proposed to me to sleep in a room adjoining theirs, divided only by a thin oaken wainscot in which one of the knots in the wood could be taken out at pleasure and thus command a full view of the nuptial couch. Clara told me she would place a pair of wax lights on a table near the bed, and out of regard to me would so manage matters that I should see all that passed between her and her handsome husband, the squire. Accordingly, we all went to bed about ten o'clock one night, and I having undressed and wrapped myself in my *robe de chambre*, placed myself on an ottoman over against the panel. Assisted by her husband, Clara was soon reduced to a state of nature and stood naked like a beautiful Eve, with her lovely hair meandering down her alabaster back and shoulders.

"Charles dear," said my sweet friend, "do you lie on the foot of the bed and let me mount you, à la St. George, you call it, I believe. I do so love that position."

'He kissed her tenderly, and being now himself naked, flung himself back on the foot of the bed.

'Then, dearest Maria, I saw, for the first time, that wondrous ivory staff with its ruby-crested head, rising from a nest of glossy black curls. Having waited a moment to give me an opportunity of seeing it, she pressed her face in his lap and took the head of his noble toy in her mouth; then after moistening it for a few seconds, she mounted astride him, displaying to my delighted gaze her large beautiful dimpled bottom and lily white thighs, between which I could clearly discern the mark of her sex; then grasping his wand in her little hand, she guided it in and immediately began to move up and down *à la postillon*.

'He clasped those white hemispheres with his hands, he squeezed them together, he held them open, he thrust his finger into the nether rosebud, he kissed her breasts, while mutual sighs of delight escaped the fond pair. As for me, I was so excited as to be almost beside myself, and felt almost suffocated. At length, I sought relief in the schoolgirl's substitute and used my finger for want of something better. Though this was but a poor expedient, it relieved the burning heat and caused a flow of love's dew, which allayed the itching desire which had taken possession of me. Meantime, Clara's climax and Charlie's came simultaneously and they lay panting in each other's arms. In a very short time, however, he was again ready for action, and making Clara kneel upon the bed he stood behind, and again the amorous encounter was renewed. Four times in various attitudes did he repeat the play, and then putting out the candles they retired to rest.

'As for me, I could scarcely sleep at all; all night I was tossing about, trying in vain with my finger to procure myself that satisfaction which I had seen her enjoy.

'Now my dear Marie, inveigh as much as you please against love; for my part the sooner some nice young fellow takes a fancy to me the better I shall like it.'

'My dearest child,' cried the dark beauty, 'I dare say it is very true that your friend has made a very excellent match and is quite happy in her husband, but what I want to impress upon you is, that for one such marriage as that, there are ten wretched ones. Besides, I will, if you like, soon demonstrate to you that there is more pleasure to be derived from the love of woman for woman than any that the male can give. We are all alone here in this lovely glen; let me show you how I will make love.'

'You!' cried the girl. 'What? Are you going then to make love to me?'

'To yourself, my pet,' whispered hoarsely the salacious woman, as her dark eyes gleamed and her hand passed up the clothes of her companion.

'Oh; but,' said the younger, 'this is very droll, good heaven, what are you about! Really, Marie, I am surprised at you.'

'Do not be surprised any longer then, my little angel,' cried her friend. 'Give me your hand,' and she passed it up her own clothes. 'Now, I will show you how to touch that little secret part. It is not by putting the finger within that the pleasure is to be gained, but by rubbing it at the top, just at the entrance; there it is that nature has placed a nerve called by doctors the clitoris, and it is this nerve which is the chief seat of bliss in our sex.' All this while the libidinous creature was manipulating with skill.

The colour came and went in the cheeks of her beauteous companion, who faintly sighed out, 'Ah, Marie, what are you doing? Oh, joy; oh blissful sensation! Ah, is it possible— oh—oh—ur—r—r.' She could no longer articulate.

The tribade saw her chance, and waited no longer; so throwing up the clothes of the young girl, she flew upon her like a panther, and forcing her face between the thighs of her friend, gamahuched her with inconceivable frenzy. Then, not satisfied with this, she pulled up her own clothes and straddled over the young girl, presenting her really

110

symmetrically formed posteriors close to her face, nearly sitting down upon it in her eagerness to feel the touch of the young girl's tongue. Nor had she to wait long; wrought up to the last pitch of lascivious extasy, her friend would have done anything she required, and now gamahuched her to her heart's desire.

I continued to watch these tribades for some time, revolving in my mind how I could get possession of the young one, for whom I had conceived a most ardent longing.

Suddenly it occurred to me that, as they were strangers in the neighbourhood, it was not likely they had walked, and that possibly, on the outskirts of the wood, I should find a coach waiting for them.

Full of designs upon the pretty young creature, I left the amorous pair to their amusement and soon reached the margin of the road. Here, ere long, I espied a coach and six with servants in rich liveries, and approaching nearer saw from the coronet on the door that it belonged to some person of quality. As I came up I accosted one of the lakeys, and tossing him a crown, asked whose carriage it was.

'His Grace the Duke of G—'s, your honour,' said the man, touching his hat respectfully as he glanced at my embroidered coat, sword and diamond buckles, and pocketing the crown.

'Then you are waiting, I presume for the two ladies in the wood?' said I.

'Yes, sir,' replied the lakey; and being a talkative, indiscreet person, he added, 'Lady Cecilia Clairville, his Grace's daughter, your honour, and Madame La Conte, her governess.'

'Ah, indeed!' said I, with as indifferent a manner as I could assume, and passed on.

At a turn of the road, I again dived into the wood and soon reached my own demesne.

'A very pretty affair, truly,' said I to myself as I took a glass of wine. Madame La Conte, engaged by the duke to complete

111

the education of his daughter, takes advantage of her position to corrupt her, and by making her a tribade renders her wretched for life; for let me tell you, Sappho, there is no more certain road to ill health, loss of beauty, pleasure, and all the zest of life, than this horrid lust for the wrong sex.

'Very well, Madame La Conte,' I soliloquised, 'I shall turn this discovery to account, you may depend'; and with that resolve I went to bed.

Next morning I sent a billet in French by a trusty messenger to his grace's mansion in Cavendish Square. It was as follows:

Madame, to all that passed between you and the lady Cecilia in the wood yesterday I was a witness. I am a man of position, and if you do not wish me to call upon the duke and acquaint him with your nefarious proceedings, you will come tomorrow afternoon at three o'clock to the big oak at the east end of the same wood, in a hackney coach, which you will alight from at the west side. To avoid discovery you had better both be masked.

Yours, as you behave yourself,

ARGUS.

Punctual to the appointment I had made, I placed myself beneath the shade of the oak, and as there was no saying what might happen, or what ambush this devil of a Frenchwoman might lay for me, I, besides my sword, put in my pocket a brace of loaded pistols. Soon the fair creatures approached, hand in hand. I raised my hat to the young girl, but as for madame, I merely honoured her with a contemptuous stare.

'Do not be alarmed, Lady Cecilia,' said I; 'you are with a man of honour, who will do you no harm. As for you, madame, you may make a friend or an enemy of me, which you will.'

'Really, monsieur,' said the governess, 'your conduct in this affair is so singular that I know not what to think; but let

112

me tell you, sir, that if you have any improper designs in inveigling us to this place, I shall know how to be avenged.'

'Doubtless, doubtless, madame; I know the French well and have well prepared for all contingencies. But allow me, ladies, to offer each an arm, and do me the honour to walk a little further into the wood.'

The alacrity with which the wily Frenchwoman complied told me at once what I had to expect.

She had resolved to assassinate me. Having made up my mind how I should act, I allowed her to lead me which way she pleased, keeping, however, a sharp look out on all sides as we strolled along. I was about to enter upon the subject of their coming, when suddenly three masked highwaymen sprang out, and demanding, 'Your money or your life,' levelled their horse pistols at us. The ladies screamed; I shook them both off, and as one of the scoundrels sent a bullet through my wig, I drew my pistols from my pocket and shot him dead; his companions then both fired, one of the bullets grazed my shoulder, but the other, curious enough, pierced the head of Madame La Conte, who, casting a glance full of fury upon me and clenching her hands, fell back a corpse.

The remaining rascals turned to flee; but before they could escape I brought down a second, and attacking the third with my sword, soon passed it through his lungs.

The enemy being now utterly defeated, I turned towards the lovely Lady Cecilia, who had fainted; and raising her light form in my arms, bore her off to the spot where the coach had been left. But it was gone. The jarvey, doubtless hearing the firing and anxious to save his skin, had driven away. My resolution was taken in a moment. So carrying my fair burthen to the nearest gate that opened into my grounds, I bore her to my secret chamber, and having fetched old Jukes and Phoebe to her assistance, with strict orders not to tell her where she was but to pay her all needful attention, I saddled a swift horse and rode off to the nearest town, one of the magistrates there being an old friend.

He was much pleased to see me, but wondered at my being covered with dust and at my sudden arrival. I told him a most dreadful affair had happened; that returning home, I heard cries for assistance in the wood, and found three ruffians robbing and ill using some ladies; that they had fired at and wounded me and killed one of the ladies; as for the other she escaped.

That in the end I had succeeded in dispatching the rascals, more in consequence of their want of skill in the use of their weapons than from any extraordinary valour on my part, and finally requesting him to give orders to have the bodies removed with a view to a coroner's inquest. All which he promised to do; and in spite of his earnest request that I should stay and drink a bottle of wine, I made my excuses and returned home.

I found my fair guest much better, and having consoled her as well as I could for the loss of Madame La Conte, I then gradually unfolded to her all the wickedness of that vile woman, and after delicately touching upon the scene in the wood the day before, I told her I had been a witness of it all and heard all the conversation.

At this dénouement, Lady Cecilia covered her face with her hands to hide her blushes; and when I enquired whether Madame La Conte had shown her my letter, she said she knew madame had received a letter, which was very unpleasant, which she tore up and burnt in a great rage, but as to its contents she was ignorant.

This was very satisfactory news for me, as my handwriting might have been recognized. So turning to the young girl with a cheerful countenance, said, laughingly, 'Well, my dear young friend, all is well that ends well; now let us make plans for the future. In the first place, it seems to me that you are formed for the joys of love. It is true I am not quite so young a lover as you might desire; but I am more fit for amorous combats than many younger men. I am rich, and though not absolutely a man of rank I am a scion of a noble house. What do you say? I know your secret. I have already seen all your charms; shall we make a match of it? Will you marry me?'

'Indeed, sir,' said the dear girl, 'your gallantry in attacking those ruffians and defending my honour would alone have been sufficient to win my heart; but as my father, the duke, has designs of wedding me to a man older than himself, an old creature whom I detest, I deem this meeting with you a most fortunate one and will accept your offer with the same ingenuous frankness with which you have made it. You say, truly, that you have already viewed my person with pleasure; take it, dear sir, and do what you please with me. I am yours forever.'

I was quite enraptured with this decision, and it being determined that the duke should be written to in the morning and informed that his daughter, entertaining an insuperable objection to the match he had in store for her, had eloped with the man of her choice.

This affair settled, and Phoebe with many sly glances having made up a bed on one of the sofas, I shut the windows and hastened to undress my future bride. She was exquisitely formed, with the most lovely breasts in the world; and as for her bottom and thighs, nothing could be finer.

We were soon in bed, and all that her finger and the wanton tongue of madame had left of her maidenhead, I soon possessed myself of. Dawn found us still in dalliance; but at length, being both quite fatigued, with a last sweet kiss we fell asleep. The next day we were to be privately married by licence.

So now, my dear Sappho, I must conclude this long letter by saying to you, 'Do thou go and do likewise.'

To Julia

Your letter, giving me an account of your adventure with the Marquis at Ranelagh Gardens, diverted me vastly. Meantime, I have not been idle.

Since you were last here, I have colonised one corner of my grounds. A discreet old creature called Jukes, has been placed in charge of that pretty cottage covered with roses and jasmine which you admired so much; and in the dairy she is assisted by the freshest and most charming of country girls. Positively you must come and pay me a visit, if only for the pleasure you will experience in the sight of Phoebe's perfections; but this is a digression and I know you hate digressions; therefore to proceed.

Phoebe and I, you must know, quite understood each other, but she is so pretty, brisk, loving and lively, and time, place and opportunity so frequently present themselves, that I have nearly killed myself with the luscious fatigue, and having fucked her in every imaginable attitude, having gamahuched her and been gamahuched in return, I at length cloyed and began to look out for some new stimulant; but alas, Madame R. did not call; I saw nothing of Mrs H. To write to them was not in accordance with my usual prudence. What was to be done? I was in despair. At this juncture, that dear old Jukes came to my aid, though very innocently, as I believe. With many curtseys and 'Hope your honour's

116

worship won't be offended at my making so bold,' etc., she told me that she would be greatly beholden if I would allow her to have an orphan grandchild of hers to live with her and Phoebe in the cottage.

She told me that her girl was a sweet pretty creature, sixteen years of age, and as she knew that I liked to amuse myself with girls sometimes (?), poor innocent soul, she thought I might like to have her.

I at once consented, and in a few days arrived one of the sweetest flowers that ever blushed unseen in the woods of Hampshire. I was charmed, and lost no time in providing suitable clothes for the little pet, and, with the aid of Phoebe, her frocks were so contrived that they only reached her knees. This, you will readily understand, was for the purpose of giving me facilities for seeing her young beauties without doing anything that might alarm her. We soon became great friends, and she took at once to Phoebe, the swing, the goldfish, strawberries and cream, the rambles in the woods, and above all her handsome new clothes; all combined to render Chloe as happy as a princess; while her old granddam would follow her exclaiming, 'Lawk a mercy! well I never!' and so on.

In the course of a few days, our young rustic had quite rubbed off her first shyness, would run in and out of my room, sit on my knee, hide my snuff box, kiss me of her own accord, and play all sorts of innocent tricks, in swinging, climbing up trees, and tumbling about on the grass; the little puss not merely showing her legs but everything else besides.

At first Mrs Jukes tried to stop it, and told her it was rude to behave so before the gentleman, but I begged she would take no notice in future as I did not mind it and liked to see the girl unrestrained and happy.

Now old Jukes always went to bed at sunset; I therefore arranged with Phoebe that after the old crone was gone to rest she should wash Chloe all over every night before putting her to bed; and that it might be done properly, I used to go and

117

witness the operation, for it gave me a pleasurable sensation to see the girl naked when Phoebe was present.

Phoebe was a clever girl and did not require much telling, so that none of the most secret charms of my little Venus were concealed from my lascivious gaze.

At one moment Phoebe would lay Chloe across her lap, giving me a full view of her dimpled bum, holding open those white globes and exposing everything beneath. Then she would lay the girl on her back and spread out her thighs, as if to dry them with the towel. In fact, she put her into almost every wanton attitude into which she had seen me place myself. The girl, meanwhile, seemed to think this washing process capital fun, and would run and skip naked about the room in the exuberance of her animal spirits.

In this amusement I found all the excitement I desired, and should perhaps have been content with viewing her beauties without attacking her innocence but for a circumstance that occurred.

One evening, after the usual performance of washing, skipping about etc., the little saucebox came and jumped on my knees, putting a leg on either side of them, and began courting a romp. Had I been a saint, whereas you know I am but a sinner, I could not have resisted such an attack on my virtue as this.

In fine, I slid my hand down and released that poor stiff prisoner, who for the last half hour had nearly burst open his prison; as a natural consequence he slid along between her thighs and his crested head appeared (as I could see by the reflection in an old mirror) impudently showing his face, between her buttocks on the rear side. She would perhaps have noticed it, were it not that my finger had long been busy in her slit already 'tickling,' she called it, and laughed heartily, tickling me under the arms in return.

Suddenly, as if the thought struck her, she said, 'Do you know that –'

She paused. Never did man wait with more exemplary

patience.

'That – that –'

Another pause.

'That I saw –'

Pause again.

'The cock –'

Here Phoebe tried to stop her, but she squeezed her interrupter's two cheeks so that she could not speak and hurriedly concluded, 'Making chickens – there.'

This was too much for my gravity, and I was convulsed with laughter; when I had a little recovered, I asked, 'And how does the cock do that, my dear?'

'Why,' said Chloe, with the most artless manner in the world, 'he tickles the hen, and when she lays eggs they come to chickens.'

'Tickles her! I do not understand,' said I.

'But he does,' insisted the girl.

'But the cock has no fingers; how can he tickle?'

'Why,' cried Chloe triumphantly, 'he has got a finger, and a long one too, and I saw it shoot from under his tail when he was treading the hen, and he tickled her, just as you are tickling me now, but putting it right into her body. Now am I not right in saying the cock makes chickens by tickling the hen?'

'Well reasoned, my little logician,' cried I, really pleased with her wit. 'I see, though, you have lived in the country, you are no fool, and I will tell you something which girls are always very curious about but which their mothers and grannies will never tell them anything of. But first tell me why you thought the cock tickling the hen made the chickens.'

'Why, because Phoebe told me, to be sure.'

'Oh, ho!' said I, laughing. 'You told her, Phoebe, did you?'

Poor Phoebe looked frightened out of her wits.

'I hope you will forgive me, sir, but Chloe did worrit so,

119

and keep all on about that ere beast of a cock that at last I up and told her.'

'God bless you, my dear girl. What if you did? There is no harm in that, I hope. There can never be anything wrong in what is natural.'

Then turning to Chloe, whose cunny I had not let go of all this while, 'Would you like to know, my dear, where the babies come from and how they are made?'

'Oh, yes: that I just should,' exclaimed Chloe, hugging and kissing me.

'Very well; now you know, I suppose, that you are not made exactly like a boy, do you not?'

'Yes, I know that down here, you mean,' and she pointed to where my finger was still tickling.

'Just so. But did you ever, by chance, happen to see a man?'

'Never.'

'And you would like to?'

'Of all things.'

'There then!' cried I, lifting her up and allowing the rampant yard to spring up against my belly.

'Oh, the funny thing!' said Chloe, then taking hold of it, 'how hot it is. That is what I have felt against my bottom these last ten minutes and could not think what it was; but what has that to do with making babies?'

'I will show you,' said I, 'but I cannot promise you that I shall make one, as I am too old for that, but it is by doing what I am going to do to Phoebe that children are begotten.'

'Oh, I see!' cried the girl, clapping her hands, 'you are going to serve Phoebe as I saw the stallion serve the mare today. That will be capital fun.'

'Serve the mare,' I ejaculated, glancing over my shoulder at Phoebe. 'How's this?'

'Well, the truth is, sir,' said the conscious girl, 'ever since your honour showed me that trick I have often gone to see them do it, and I was watching them today when she came

120

running into the stable. So I was obliged to tell her all about it, as I did about the chickens.'

'Well,' said I, 'if she has seen that, I see no harm in her seeing the other; so pull up your clothes, my dearest creature.'

In a moment Phoebe had tucked up her petticoats, and kneeling on the truckle bed and jutting her white posteriors well out, presented a full view of all her charms.

'Oh, my,' cried Chloe, 'why Phoebe, you have got hair growing on your –'

She stopped, with a charming blush, hid her face in my bosom.

'And so will you have,' I whispered, 'but now observe what I am going to do, and mind you tickle me underneath all the while.'

This she did in the most delightful manner, occasionally laughing to see Phoebe wriggling about. As soon as all was over, I sent Phoebe to my room for some refreshments and wine, and while she was gone I gamahuched the lovely Chloe, which operation, coming as it did after all the frigging she had undergone, roused at once her dormant passions into precocious energy. With eagerness she seized my again erect wand, and putting it into her mouth, worked it up and down so that, just as Phoebe returned, I sent a spirting shower over her tongue while her virgin dew drenched my own.

'Oh, my! how salty it is,' sputtered the girl, spitting and making a wry face.

'And is it that stuff sir, that makes the babies?'

'One drop of it, my dear, is sufficient to make a girl as pretty as you.'

'Or a boy?'

'Yes, or a boy.'

After supper, Chloe wanted Phoebe and me to perform again, but I told her that was quite enough for one night and that she was on no account to say anything of what she had seen to her granddam.

Now I think my dear Julia will say I have related a most interesting adventure; but really, I wish you would come and stay a few days and share in our sports. I shall confidently expect to see you before long.

To Euphrosyne

Your pretty cousin Sappho will doubtless have told you the startling news, that I am – what do you think? – married! It is true, however, and a very charming little creature my wife is, I can tell you.

Quite free from all those silly notions of propriety and jealousy, her chief delight is to make me happy, not only by giving up to me her own pretty person but by throwing in my way any chance that may occur when there is any new face that pleases me.

With this view, she proposed to me that we should adopt the two daughters of a cousin of hers who, being poor, accepted a situation in the East India Company's service, and having subsequently contracted in the East an imprudent marriage, these children were the fruits of it. Their mother being dead, he sent them home to be educated; and by a singular chance they were placed at the school of Mrs J., who you know is a tenant of mine and occupies that house near this place which I offered to your papa some years ago.

Of course, after my marriage I presented Cecilia to my household as their mistress, no object being gained by keeping it a secret; and there is a great convenience in this, as whatever they may have thought before about the secret chamber and grounds, as my wife is now with me it silences scandal at once. Now I will go on to relate to you the acquisition this plan of my wife's has produced.

We drove over to Mrs J., with whom I was always a favourite; and with reason, as more than once when she was a little straitened for her rent I have sent her a receipt for the money without ever receiving it.

She is the widow of a naval officer, and though over five and thirty years of age, has still the remains of considerable personal attractions.

She was at home and delighted with our visit. So we opened the object of it.

'My dear Mrs J.,' began Lady Cecilia with the smile of a seraph, 'I have persuaded Sir Charles to allow me to adopt my poor cousin's girls, and I now intend to take the entire charge of these young ladies.'

Then observing Mrs J. began to look very thoughtful, she quickly added, 'But do not misundertand me. I mean not to remove them from your excellent supervision; their education must of course proceed as usual. All I want is permission to break through one of your rules and ask you to let them come and pass a few days with us sometimes, instead of coming for the regular holidays.'

'I am sure,' cried Mrs J., whose countenance had quite cleared up during this speech, 'I shall be vastly pleased to oblige your ladyship in any way in my power. Pray arrange it just as you like.'

'And if,' added I, 'my dear Mrs J., you will yourself occasionally favour us with your company and bring any of your young ladies with you, we shall both, I am sure, be enchanted. You know I have some pretty grounds to which I do not admit everybody, but your name will be an "open sesame" at all times.'

'Oh, Sir Charles,' cried the good lady with a conscious blush (which showed she knew those precincts well), 'you are too good, I am sure. But really, to tell you the truth, I was quite frightened when I saw your carriage drive up the avenue, as I remembered there are two quarters' rent in arrear; indeed, I am afraid you find me a sorry tenant.'

'I would not change you, my dear madam, for all the best tenants in the world. But see, I anticipated your fears, well knowing the sensibility of your nature and your honourable sentiments; here is the receipt, and as for the money, pray accept it to procure any little article of jewellery you may require.'

Mrs J. glanced furtively at my wife before she replied; but seeing nothing in that sweet face but the most amiable and charming smile she said at once, 'Oh, Sir Charles! how very considerate and kind you are; always the same noble gentleman, madam,' she continued, turning to Lady Cecilia, 'so kind, so generous.'

'Then it is all settled,' said Cecilia; 'and remember to bring some of the prettiest of your young ladies. You know Sir Charles loves a good romp with young girls, and I am not at all jealous.'

'Oh, my lady, I can see you are a sweet creature, and I am delighted Sir Charles has made such a happy choice. I will bring two or three of my girls with your dear cousins; but will you not see them before you go?'

'Oh, yes, certainly; send for them, I beg.'

Mrs J. rang the bell, and presently appeared two of the most lovely, blooming girls I had ever seen. Augusta and Agnes they were called, one sixteen and the other seventeen years old. They had the sweetest and most innocent countenances in the world, and their manners did ample justice to Mrs J.'s training. I took one on each knee, and as I kissed their rosy cheeks I felt over their muslin frocks that they had each nice, firm, plump little bottoms, with which I hoped ere long to be better acquainted.

Mrs J. saw the movement, and smiled archly. Then catching Cecilia's eye, 'A sad man! a sad rake! is he not, my lady?'

'Oh, indeed he is!' cried Cecilia, laughing; 'and if I mistake not, you and I know all about it, *n'est-ce pas?*'

125

Mrs J. blushed scarlet, but seeing that the remark was mere playful badinage and not malicious, she soon recovered her presence of mind. After a merry chat with the girls and the tip of a guinea a piece we took our leave.

As soon as we were in the carriage my wife gave me a tap with her fan, saying, 'Positively, Charles, you are incorrigible; I do verily believe that Mrs J. is an old flame of yours.'

'Of course she is, my love; and a deuced fine woman she was, I can assure you; a little stale now, perhaps, but a most useful person, and so prudent. Whenever she has had any orphan girls, or girls whose friends did not pay well or punctually, if they were pretty (and she will not take ugly ones), she has always brought them to me; and in this way for five guineas I have bought many a maidenhead of her. Yet so cleverly has she managed matters that nothing unpleasant has ever arisen out of these affairs. There was one case, indeed, which I had almost forgotten, which was rather awkward, as the fool of a guardian thought proper to take offence upon his ward complaining to him; and he came down here in a towering passion with Frank Firebrace of the Guards. He waited in the wood and sent the captain to me with a cartel.

'I was not the man to refuse such a summons, but told him he must wait till I also sent for a friend.

'I knew where an old chum of mine was to be found and posted off a messenger for him. On his arrival we started to the place of rendezvous, and there, on that deep dell which you admire so much, I was under the disagreeable necessity of dispatching the guardian of the girl. Egad, it was a deuced unpleasant business and made poor Mrs J. very much afraid of Bridewell, at the time.'

'Oh! dear Charles,' said Cecilia, 'how charmingly wicked you are, and vastly cool too you seem to speak of it.'

'Do not let us speak of it any more; it was one of those contretemps which occasionally mar the uniform career of a man of pleasure.'

'Really, Charles, you quite frighten me with your coolness. But never mind, you dear man, I love you with all my heart and shall never think very harshly of your little peccadilloes.'

The following Thursday brought Mrs J., the two young cousins, and three other young ladies about whom it will be necessary to say a few words.

Miss Marshall was a poor Irish girl from the county of Kerry, whose unnatural father, a naval officer, having placed her three years before with Mrs J., had never paid a shilling, and upon writing to the town where she came from she found that her father was her only relative in the world. Mrs J. looked upon her, therefore, as lawful prey.

This girl was a thorough Irish beauty, with dark blue eyes and black hair, a rather dingy skin, a pretty enough face, and having a well-formed figure, though rather thin; however, there was something taking about her, although she looked grave and sad. She was turned eighteen years old.

The next I shall describe was Miss Jennings, a merry laughing blonde, very plump and pretty, with a profusion of light hair. She had been brought up by her grandmother, who paid very little. This girl was also about eighteen and ripe for a frolic.

The last of the trio, Miss Bellew, was a tall, handsome girl of nineteen, nicely made, but a little too slight if anything. She was dark and swarthy, a brunette, in fact; but there was soul in her black eyes, and withal a look of languor quite enchanting.

Such being our party, and chocolate and fruit with plenty of cakes and bonbons being served on the lawn by Phoebe and Chloe, we all soon became great friends. The refection concluded, and leaving Cecilia to entertain Mrs J., I took the bevy of girls to see the poultry yard and then the ponies. I had previously given Phoebe a hint to let the stallion into the mare's compartment, so that when we arrived the animals were in the very act – a sight which provoked the astonishment and laughter of the girls and made Miss

Marshall look very pale and grave while Misses Jennings and Bellew blushed up to the eyes.

'Oh, come away, come away,' cried Miss Marshall, turning sharp round; but I stopped her.

'Why should they go away, my dear?' I asked.

'Because, because –' and then stopped.

'Because what?' said I.

'Because – I think you are a naughty bad man, Sir Charles,' sobbed the foolish girl, and burst into tears.

'Oh Bella,' cried all the other girls in a breath, 'for shame, to speak so to Sir Charles. Never mind her, sir, she is always like that, a miserable thing to spoil fun.'

'I am sorry to hear it,' said I. 'When I invite young ladies here I expect them to be cheerful and polite, and if they are not we have a birch rod quite handy.'

Mrs J. coming up at this moment, the girls all ran to tell her how Bella had behaved.

'In that case, Sir Charles,' said the good lady, 'we must commence the sports by giving her a good flogging.'

Miss Marshall turned paler than she was before at this announcement.

Mrs J. had a heavy hand, as she knew by dear bought experience, but she was of a dogged and sulky dispostion and said nothing.

'How now, miss,' cried Mrs J., 'say you are very sorry immediately or you shall be flogged at once.'

No answer.

'Will you apologise or not?'

No answer.

'Yes, yes; I see we must make you speak then. Here, my good girl,' said she, addressing Phoebe. 'You are strong, take her up, and you, my lasses, come, hold her legs.'

And the refractory Bella being mounted, and her clothes thrown over her head, Mrs J. selected from a new birch broom a goodly handful of twigs, and tying them with a ribband prepared for action.

We all now had a full view of her well-formed white buttocks and thighs; and the other girls, who seemed to enjoy the scene, held her legs so wide apart that we could see her pouting cunny and all the regions thereabout.

Bella, meanwhile, bounding and struggling to be free, only exposed her charms the more.

'Now,' said Mrs J., 'you young hussy, for whom I have never yet received a shilling, I'll teach you manners, you wretched pauper, I will.'

And she commenced flogging her till the stubborn girl roared for mercy and her white bottom glowed again.

'No – no – no,' cried Mrs J., giving a tremendous cut each time she said the word, 'I will flog this devil out of you before I have done.'

'Oh, dear madam, pray forgive me. Oh – oh – oh – oh; kind Sir Charles, do intercede! Oh, I shall die; oh! oh!'

But by this time I had got too much interested to interfere and quieted Cecilia with a gesture, and the operation proceeded.

But at the sight of the poor girl I relented, and lifting her up bore her to a couch in my room; and having unfastened her dress and bathed her temples with Hungary water, I left her and returned to my company. Preparations were just being made for a game of hunt-the-slipper, and every one being seated on the lawn I ran round the circle, every now and then feeling for the slipper under the legs of the girls.

The little screams, the shouts of laughter, and the fun was tremendous; for you may be sure that every girl in her turn felt my hand between her naked thighs.

With some it was a hasty grasp, but with others I lingered and fairly frigged, pretending all the while that I was sure they had the slipper. To see Agnes and Augusta laugh at being tickled was delightful; and the conscious blushes of the misses Jennings and Bellew were equally enchanting. As for Miss Bellew, her languishing black eyes shot forth scintillations of light as she fairly spent in my hand; but Jennings was less precocious and merely laughed at the fun.

Altogether it was a most fucktious romp, and made me so amorous that I at length proposed a game of hide-and-seek for a change, and unperceived beckoned to Cecilia; we both ran to hide.

Having retired into a deep cluster of trees and shrubs, I put my wife on her knees and was into her in a moment, at the same time calling out 'whoop.' Into the wood they all came shouting and laughing, but could not for a long time find us; at length Agnes and Augusta taking an opposite vista to their companions, came suddenly upon us just as my climax came. I immediately drew out, and thus gave them a complete view of that red headed staff, at the sight of which, and of their cousin's ivory posteriors shining in the sun, they stopped, turned round, and bounded off to their companions, crying out:

'Oh! Miss Jennings, oh Miss Bellew, here's Sir Charles doing to cousin Cecilia just what the horse did to the mare!'

Then we heard a whispering; and presently I became aware, by the rustling of the branches, that the girls were placing themselves in ambush to see all they could.

The idea of such beauteous spectators brought me up to the mark again in a moment, and at it we went in good style. Every now and then an eager face would peep out from among the leaves and then be withdrawn in great trepidation, which caused such a thrill to run through my veins that I brought that second embrace to a conclusion much sooner than I had a mind to.

No sooner did they see that I was beginning to button up again but they scampered off in different directions, pretending to be looking for us. Meanwhile, we shifted our quarters and again cried out 'whoop.'

This time they ran up to catch us, pretending, the little sly pussies, that they had had such a hunt for us. Being now Miss Bellew's turn to hide, we all remained on the lawn while she ran into the wood. It now occurred to me for the first time that Mrs J. and Phoebe had disappeared, not could I anywhere see Chloe.

So that when Miss Bellew's 'whoop' summoned us to the
wood, instead of looking for her I hunted in every direction
for the truants, and at length, at some distance from the spot
where the game was going on, I fancied I saw a bit of blue silk
between the trees; and bending my steps to a thick clump of
hazel I approached softly, and lo, on a little patch of mossy
turf, in a hollow space, I espied the excellent lady doing a
little bit of tribadism with Phoebe. They were at the height
of enjoyment; Phoebe uppermost.

'Ah, ah, my sweet girl,' Mrs J. was sighing out. 'That is it.
Ah, now you've found the right place, at the – top. Oh, bliss;
ah-oh. Ur-r-r! oh, how nice; continue to roll your tongue
round and round.'

Then slapping the beautiful great white bottom of Phoebe,
which was presented to her, she continued, 'Oh, what
heavenly charms, what a skin! what glorious white globes!
what a delicious little nether mouth, let me kiss your sweet
cunny; let me thrust my tongue in and taste your spendings.
Ah, this is bliss indeed, Ur-r-r-r!'

Then Phoebe began.

'Ah, dear madam, what are you doing? oh lud, it do make
me feel so funny loike. Oh, my ain't it nice though? Oh –'

A gushing of spending from Mrs J. stopped her mouth,
while the movements became furious. Phoebe rolled off on to
the grass and the two women lay without sense or motion
beyond the heaving of their breasts. I was much amused and
retreated without being discovered.

I now thought of Chloe, and wanting my snuffbox which I
had left indoors, I went for it, when the first thing that met
my eyes was the girl trying to console the naughty Miss
Marshall, who was lying on her side on a couch, with her face
to the wall, while the good-natured Chloe was bathing the
poor flayed bum of the young lady.

I approached softly, and with my finger on my lip
motioned to Chloe to take no notice, and seated myself about

a yard from them.

As Miss Marshall's clothes were turned up above her waist, I was able to contemplate at my ease the symmetrical proportions of her sylph-like form.

The fine contour of her virgin rose and the little rose bud attached thereto all was before me.

Presently she spoke. 'How kind you are to me, dearest Chloe,' she said, languidly. 'I begin to feel in less pain now, but what is very singular, I, who never had any sensations in that part before, now feel a most singular itching between my legs – in the slit, you know.'

'Just here?' cried Chloe, laughing and putting her finger in.

'Oh yes, yes. Ah, how nice it feels now you touch it. Oh, I feel so ashamed,' and she covered her face with her hand.

Chloe withdrew her hand.

'I did not mean to offend you,' she said.

'Offend me; oh, no. Let me feel that dear little finger again.'

I approached on my hands and knees and quickly substituted my finger for Chloe's.

'Oh, my dear girl,' she cried, 'oh, how very nice, but I feel quite ashamed.'

Then, as I touched her clitoris, a shiver ran through her frame. She threw herself over on her back, expanded her thighs, and, with her eyes still closed, murmured, 'Come, come here, darling girl, on my bosom, on my bosom.'

I placed Chloe there in a moment, and then tossing up the girl's clothes, I began toying with her lovely buttocks. Then, kneeling up behind her, I directed my fiery steed straight at Miss Marshall's maidenhead.

The first push took me in about an inch, but, with a shriek and a start, the Irish girl opened her eyes, commencing with, 'Oh, my dear Chloe, how you hurt me, I –'

Then seeing me she struggled to get up and turned pale with terror.

'Oh, for heaven's sake, let me get up – oh, goodness! Mercy! mercy!'

These ejaculations followed every thrust, for I would not let go but made Chloe lie with all her weight on the Marshall until I was at length fairly into her body. Then, indeed, I rolled Chloe on one side and extending myself on the bosom of the girl and grasping her tightly in my arms I consummated the defloration.

At first angry, she finished by hugging her ravisher in her arms and covering him with kisses.

All this, which has taken so long to tell, happened in an incredibly short space of time, so that I was hardly missed ere I reappeared among my young friends.

Mrs J. and Phoebe now joined us, looking very innocent, and I having interceded for Miss Marshall, she and Chloe were sent for and joined in the sports. I had quite tamed the angry petulant girl and she occasionally glanced at me with a look full of meaning and of indefinable tenderness. Her passions were aroused and she had tasted of the tree of knowledge.

It being now eight o'clock, supper was served up to us with a profusion of all the delicacies of the season and the choicest wines and liqueurs. After this we had a dance and a game of blindman's buff, and then my guests took their departure, Mrs J. declaring that she had never enjoyed herself more! (Glancing at Phoebe.)

'Well then,' said I, 'suppose you all come again next Thursday?'

'Oh, I shall be enchanted, I am sure, to do so, Sir Charles,' said Mrs J., 'but I suppose you will not want to see Miss Marshall any more?'

'On the contrary,' I remarked, 'she has quite made the *amende honorable*, and we are now very good friends. Is it not so, young lady?' I added, turning to her.

A burning blush suffused her pale face, but she managed to stammer out, 'Oh, yes, Madame, I am sure Sir Charles is most kind. I am very sorry I behaved as I did, but if you will let me come next time I promise never so to offend again, even if there are fifty horses and mares instead of one.'

With that I kissed them all round, and handing them into my coach bid them good night.

Adieu, dear friend.

To Lais

Lady Cecilia has fallen in love, and with a very Daphnis too, the beautiful brother of the charming Phoebe. He came here the other day to see his sister, and prodigiously took the fancy of my lady. As we are far too philosophical, in this our terrestrial paradise, to agitate ourselves with such absurd passions as jealousy, I left Cecilia to do as she liked; so she has engaged the pretty fellow, who is just sixteen and the image of his sister, as her body page, but instead of putting him in livery, has dressed him à la Watteau, a style of costume at once simple and elegant.

Of course, she made his sister give him a good scrubbing and combing before he mounted his new clothes, and now powdered, perfumed, and dressed he looks fit for a princess. Phoebe is hugely pleased that Jack is to stay here, and as for Chloe, she evidently has some very sinister designs on his virtue.

I told Cecilia that I congratulated her on such an acquisition and hoped she would not object to my seeing some of the performances. She laughed, and replied, 'Oh, see all you like, my dear Charles, only don't let the boy know at first, as he is very bashful and timid.'

I promised compliance.

A few days afterwards, as I lay on the banks of the lake listlessly feeding the carp, Phoebe came running to me, and having seated herself quite out of breath by my side, she told me that Cecilia and her brother were amusing themselves in the grotto, in the grove of beeches, and if I would make haste I might see something that would amuse me. So, throwing my arm round Phoebe's waist, I accompanied her, going round to the opposite side to the entrance. We looked through a chink in the rockwork and could both see and hear all that passed.

First I observed Cecilia seated on the mossy bank, and holding the boy, whose breeches were down, between her naked thighs, his hands were toying with her bubbies.

While she, having tucked up his fine cambric shirt, with her right hand caressed his little stiff thing and with her left patted his soft and girlish bottom.

'Oh, you dear fellow,' said she, 'what a beautiful figure you have got, your waist is so small, your bottom so plump, dimpled, and rounded, and your skin so soft; you have such a lovely face, your hair is so silky luxuriant, and beautiful, and you have such little hands and feet, surely nature quite intended you for a girl, only she gave you this little saucy cock instead of something else, which, however, I am very glad of, as you will be able to play with me. Dear boy, do you like me to tickle it?'

'Oh, yes, my lady,' cried the lad, 'very much indeed, and I do love these little breasts so, do let me kiss them.'

And pulling her bubbies out he buried his face between them.

'But,' she exclaimed, 'you have not looked at this other little secret place – but perhaps, you have seen girls before?'

'Why, my lady, to say the truth, I have, but only little ones. I should like to see your ladyship's beautiful cunt very much.'

'Oh, fie, naughty boy, do not use such naughty words. But look, here it is.'

And she straddled open her legs.

'Feel it with your hand. Oh, you dear fellow, that is nice;

136

now lie down upon me and I will show you what love is.'

And grasping his beautiful buttocks, she drew him to her and he slipped in with ease.

'Now, dear boy, move up and down, that's it, my stallion; you are, I see, an apt pupil.'

Then holding open those white hemispheres, she inserted her delicate finger into his little rosy orifice behind, and entwining her lovely limbs round his loins, they were presently bounding and heaving with delight.

The sight was so exhilarating to both Phoebe and myself that I lifted up her clothes, and still contemplating the ardent young lovers, commenced the same game myself.

Now, whatever the ancients may have thought on the subject, I must confess I have never seen what the peculiar point of attraction could be in having beautiful boys, as they unquestionably did; yet when I saw that lovely young bottom bounding up and down, and Cecilia's wanton finger frigging away, a strange dizziness seized me and I felt a lust, stronger than the lust for women, lay hold of me.

But one cannot be perfectly happy in this world long together, so that it happened that just at the height of titillation, my climax came and I sent a gushing stream into her bowels.

Cecilia and her Daphnis having also died away in bliss, we beat a retreat, to prevent discovery.

Thus you see, my dear Lais, that like a true Epicurean, I never let slip any pleasure within my reach.

I think it behoves us to live while we may and give full scope to those delicious sensual appetites which we can only enjoy for so short a time.

Hoping soon to have the happiness of seeing you here,

I remain,
Your devoted Admirer.

To Thalia

I believe, my dear girl, I gave you a full relation of all that had passed here during this last three months on the occasion of that delicious clandestine visit you paid me about a week ago. I am now going to continue the narrative, which I hope will prove edifying to my dear girl.

You must know then, my love, that I was most anxious to become better acquainted with my wife's cousins, and as she was quite willing I should do just as I liked with them, I sent a letter to Mrs J. requesting that they might pass a few days with us. They arrived accordingly the next morning.

'Now, Cecilia,' said I, 'I want you to leave us entirely to ourselves; so do you go and make a few calls in the neighbourhood.'

To this the dear wife at once consented, so taking each of my cousins by the hand, I proposed we should go a nutting (you know what a famous nut wood I have here). The girls were delighted and skipped merrily along. Arrived at the wood, they began climbing the trees in search of the nuts, showing me their fat bottoms and legs without the least concern.

As soon as they had gathered a pretty considerable basketful, I proposed that we should seat ourselves under a spreading tree and eat them.

'Now, my loves,' said I, 'while you are cracking your

nuts, I will try and amuse you.'

The pretty creatures in seating themselves drew up their legs so as to make a lap to hold their nuts, and as Mrs J. had taken care their petticoats should be short, I had a full view of all their youthful charms. Plump, white thighs, between which pouted their rosy slits, a luscious sight, enough to fire the veins of an anchorite.

But, as I have no pretensions to that holy character, I was beside myself with desire and ready to eat them up altogether. However, I restrained my impatience with much ado and began to beat about the bush.

'Now I daresay, my darlings, you would like to know where the babies come from?'

'Oh!' cried Agnes, 'I know very well.'

Then whispering mysteriously in my ear, 'They come out of the parsley bed.'

'Nonsense,' cried Augusta, who had overheard her, 'no such thing, I know better than that; they come from the mother, do they not, Sir Charles?'

'Yes, my dear,' said I sententiously, 'indeed they do; but can you tell me how they got into the mother's stomach in the first place, and how they get out in the second?'

'Why, no, Sir Charles, I cannot tell what made them get there, not do I exactly know how they come into the world; some of the girls at our school say that the mother's stomach opens and lets them out, but I really do not quite know.'

'Would you like me to tell you, then?'

'Oh, dear sir, of all things, do, do, tell us all about it.'

'Well, then,' said I laughing, 'I must begin at the beginning.'

'Yes, yes, that's it,' cried the girls in a breath cracking their nuts and very wickedly throwing the shells at an unoffending sparrow who was hopping about near them.

'Very well,' said I. 'In the beginning the heaven and the earth were created –'

'Oh, lud, we know all about that, you see. But what has

139

that got to do with it?' cried the saucy Augusta.

'In the beginning the heaven and the earth were created,' I went on dogmatically, 'every creeping thing and all that therein is, male and female. Now, can you tell me why they were made male and female?'

My pupils looked puzzled.

'I will tell you,' said I gravely, 'they were made male and female that they may be joined together, just as you saw the pony stallion and the mare joined, and thus propagate their kind. There is nothing wrong or indelicate in their doing this; are we not told to be "fruitful and multiply"?'

'Of course we are,' cried the girls in a breath.

'Well, then,' I continued, 'Miss Marshall was wrong in wishing you to come away the other day, for, my dear children, you were contemplating one of the works of nature. Now you know, I daresay, that boys are not made like girls?'

'Oh, yes; we know that.'

'Well, shall I tell you why they are not?'

'Oh, yes; do, do.'

'Well then, because that innocent thing of the boy's is capable, in the man, of becoming a great thing, and nature has ordained that he shall feel a particular pleasure in putting that part of him into that female opening, of which I see two specimens before me.'

They both blushed and pulled down their clothes.

'When it is in, he moves up and down, and in doing so gives great pleasure to the female, and after a time he discharges into her a thick milky, or rather gruel-like, fluid, which is the seed; this being received into the womb and fecundating the ovaries or eggs, which are in her fallopian tubes – so called from a learned doctor named Fallopius, who discovered them – the egg descends into the womb and begins to grow, and nine months later a child is born.'

'Oh, but that is very funny, and very wonderful,' they cried.

'My dear girls, it is not funny, but it is wonderful.'

They both looked very thoughtful; at length Augusta said, 'And would there be any harm in your showing us what this wonderful thing which makes the babies is like?'

'On the contrary, my dear girl, here it is!' and unbuttoning my breeches, out sprung my truncheon as stiff as a carrot.

'Oh, gracious, what a funny thing,' was the ejaculation which escaped them as they approached and began to handle Mr Pasquin.

'That is the true maker of babies, my darlings, is he not a fine dolly? Play with him a little and soon you will see what the seed is like, and remember every drop may contain a baby.'

'Oh, the funny, big, red-headed thing,' exclaimed the girls, rubbing and pulling it about. 'And what are these two balls for, Sir Charles?'

'They, my dears, contain the seed, which is formed in the loins at first, and then descending through those balls pass into the woman.'

'Then,' said Augusta, 'when people are said to be in love, it means that they want to join those parts together.'

'Just so, that is the end of all marriages.'

'But,' argued Agnes, 'do ladies really like to have it done to them?'

'Of course they do, my dear, if they love the man they marry.'

'But why do they like it?'

'Because they feel a strange pleasure in the act.'

'Really, how very odd,' both exclaimed.

'Not at all,' said I, 'let me just tickle you a little in that part and you will soon know what I mean.'

'Indeed,' said Augusta, 'I know already, for when you did that to me while playing hunt-the-slipper, I thought it very nice.'

At this admission, as they had not ceased caressing that great erect prick, a *jet d'eau* spouted forth, covering both their hands with the warm fluid, at which they both gave a little scream of astonishment and then fell examining it attentively.

'And every drop of this curious stuff contains a baby?' enquired Augusta.

'Every drop,' said I.

'Who would have thought it,' she continued, much interested, 'how very, very curious.'

'Having now told you all about that part of the business, my dear girls,' said I, 'I must now go on to tell you that the pleasures of love are manifold, and I will explain to you what some of those pleasures are.

'First of all, is the pleasure derived from titillation with the finger, as practised by school-girls. But this, though very exquisite when first commenced, palls after a year or two, deadens the sensation of the little cunny and, what is worse, injures the health. The blooming cheeks will then become pale, the bright eyes sunken, the skin yellow and flabby. Therefore that is not the enjoyment I intend to recommend to you, my dears.

'Secondly, there is tribadism, or the love of one girl for another, which leads them mutually to gratify each other's desires by kissing and licking that salacious part of their bodies. No doubt the bliss is great, but I never yet met a girl who would assert that a tribade could satisfy her. It is very exciting, no doubt, but after working the nervous sensibility up to the highest tension, it leaves you still tingling with desire – longing, wishing for something you know not what, but forever unsatisfied. Like that unhappy Tantalus, forever plunged to the chin in water but unable to drink; so I cannot recommend tribadism.

'Thirdly, there is the true and right kind of bliss, when two young creatures of opposite sexes meet, kiss, caress, and coo; and time, place, and opportunity occurring, join together those luscious parts of their persons. Add to this the pursuit of pleasure *en règle*, and to these delights of love I will introduce you.'

The girls, who had paid great attention, came nestling up to me, saying, 'Oh, what a dear, nice man you are, Sir

Charles; I do love you so very much, you are so kind.'

I kissed them both, and with my two hands patting each of their peach-like nether beauties, while they played with dolly of the red head, I continued, 'But before I introduce you to your young lover that is to be, I want to say a few words on incentives. Now, while I disapprove of fingering, tribadism, gamahuching, and the like when intended as a sole means of satisfying natural lust, I think such acts may be practised if the natural completion in a hearty fuck is to follow.

'None of these acts will then do you the least harm, because the effect of fucking is to tranquillize the nerves and produce a delicious calmness and serenity. Having now, therefore, concluded my sermon, I will go without delay and find Master Jack, who I am very sure is up to some mischief, either stealing my peaches or fighting among the cocks in the poultry yard, setting the dogs at old Mother Jukes' cat, or teasing Chloe. However, I will bring him captive to your feet.'

I found our young Daphnis at the cottage. But let me describe him to you, for you did not see him when here.

You are to imagine then, a beautiful young girl, but with male, instead of female, attributes, with a polished skin like alabaster, and whose exquisite face is a perfect oval; imagine a girl of sixteen with large melting eyes, black lashes, pencilled eyebrows, *nez retroussé*, small coral-lipped mouth, teeth like pearls, and dimpled cheeks tinted with the softest blush of the rose.

Imagine a profusion of light brown curling hair, powdered and tied by a cherry-coloured ribbon, rather narrow chest, small waist, and voluptuous hips and accessories; in fine a charming picture full of grace and elegance, dressed à la Watteau.

I found the young rascal lying at the foot of a cherry tree, up which Chloe had clambered, lazily eating the fruit she threw down to him, while ever and anon he languidly raised his eyes to look at that other fruit which her short dress

143

rendered so conspicuous.

As I conducted him into the nut wood, the two sweet girls ran to meet us, and then looked shy, shook their shoulders and blushed. Not so the boy; he went up to them with some gallant speech or other not now worth repeating, and soon they were at high romps on the grass, to my great delight. After a little more of this by-play, he began to take all sorts of liberties.

They retaliated, so that, in a quarter of an hour, the acquaintance was so far improved that they had got his breeches off, his shirt up above his waist; then Augusta falling over the root of a tree, up went her legs; he fell upon her, and then – then at it he went in good style, Agnes behind him tickling his marbles and Augusta hugging and kissing him with all her strength.

The sight was most fucktious. His beautiful girlish bottom bounding up and down, its peach-like cheeks trembling from their very plumpness, his stiff cock, now in, now out; her plump thighs shining white against the greensward and her lovely shaped, mossy cunny. Add to this the various beauties her sister also displayed, and I think you will admit that a lovelier picture could not well be conceived, and I would have given fifty guineas to have had Watteau here at that moment to paint the scene.

At this enchanting moment, seeing Phoebe crossing a neighbouring copse, I called her, and putting her on all fours she soon became a performer in this *fête champêtre*. She bounded and wriggled, I thrust; the youngsters shouted and laughed. Sure there never was such a merry luscious scene. But as all things, even the most delightful, must have an end, and Phoebe had been very skillfully manipulating me for some minutes, amidst ah's and oh's and Oh my dear love's, and sighs and coos of delirious bliss, she died away in extasy. Nor were the young ones long after us. As for Augusta, she fairly ground her teeth in joy.

To Helen

What an age it seems, beloved Helen, since I last saw your sylph-like form enlivening these shades. The very trees seem to droop in your absence. Cannot you come and pass a few days with us? When I think of the austere, cold-hearted man they have married you to, I feel oppressed with a sadness which no delights can dispel. Come then, my lovely Helen, and rejoice me with a view of your charms once more.

You ask me for news of our doings here; and though I have always some new adventure to relate, I should do so with more pleasure could I but identify you with this paradise.

Cecilia and I diversify our amusements. To this end she has the most cavalier servant in the world, and I two sweet girls who are entirely at my disposal.

I wish you could see Phoebe and Chloe, for you would scarcely find anywhere more lovely creatures.

Then there are my wife's cousins, Augusta and Agnes, who come sometimes, and who I have initiated in all the mysteries of Venus.

Yesterday we had a garden party, consisting of Mrs J. and three of her pupils, Mesdames Bellew, Marshall, and Jennings, besides the cousins.

The sports consisted of swinging, blind-man's-buff, hunt-the-slipper, hide-and-seek, and concluded with a bath in the lake and supper on the lawn.

My new swing was hailed with acclamations by the young ladies, who with Chloe and Phoebe, not forgetting Lady Cecilia, were speedily seated therein. This filled up every seat, which relieved Mrs J., poor woman, as she had no desire, she said, to make an exhibition of herself at her age. And *entre nous*, she is a little *passé*, and has, besides, such a tremendous black bearskin in a certain quarter that the sight of so grim an affair would have spoiled the view. As for our Daphnis (that is his *nom d'amour*, you know, otherwise he rejoices in the vulgar epithet of 'Jack'), he was in raptures and ran along the line of beauty trying to see all he could. Then, oh, the laughter, the little screams, the coquettish attempts to prevent him seeing their charms, and the badinage and saucy jokes that were bandied about, made up a scene which quite beggars description. Then as soon as the swing began to move and swung high in the air, the fun grew fast and furious and the sight was not only exciting but almost singular; for as I sat underneath, as they swung over my head, I could not see anything but bottoms, thighs, legs, and pretty feet, all of a row. Occasionally, to obtain a firmer seat, one of them would give a wriggle or twist, which showed me some new charm – a nymphoe or clitoris would pop out – and with each movement I discovered new beauties. When they were tired of this fun, we played blind-man's-buff, I of course being blind man. The little pussies were pretty rough in their play, pushing me about at their pleasure and taking all manner of liberties; but no sooner had I caught one of them but I took my revenge, putting my hand up her clothes without ceremony. Feeling a luscious pouting little cunny, on which sprouts a soft down, I at once recognized it and cried out, 'Ah! I know you, it is Miss Bellew.'

'Right, right!' shouted the merry voices, and pulling off the handkerchief I at once made her pay toll before them all. You will observe we went far beyond kissing here. In fact, tossing up the young lady's petticoats, I pushed her gently on her hands and knees, and having long been primed was into her in a moment. As for the others, with many a gay repartee, they seated themselves in a circle and watched the performance.

Poor Miss Bellew, as you may suppose (though nothing loth to the thing itself), would have preferred a more private place. But seeing there was no escape, she submitted with a good grace. Indeed, she need not have distressed herself, for her companions, stimulated by what they saw, were soon so fully occupied themselves as to pay little attention to us. Cecilia led Daphnis into a little grove, sacred to Priapus; Phoebe and Mrs J. disappeared down an avenue; Augusta and Chloe became tribades for the time; while the others were all frigging away right and left.

Sure the isle of Capri in the days of Tiberius could have shown no more voluptuous scenes than those which startled the very birds in the trees from their propriety.

But, alas! this is but a terrestrial Elysium, and we soon found that we were neither gods nor goddesses. Half an hour satisfied all our desires for that bout, and all were soon seated for a game of hunt-the-slipper, which passed off with the usual pleasantries of frigging and feeling, in which I allowed Daphnis to share, and the young wag set us all in a roar by insisting that as he could not find the slipper he was sure Mrs J. had put it up her cunt, and in spite of all her protestations he would feel for himself, which I have no doubt that cunning and salacious dame relished most heartily.

You must know, my love, that Mrs J. is still a fine woman, who, ten or twelve years ago, has often had me panting on her bosom. Phew! those days are gone by; I require younger stuff to give me a stiffener now. Then came the romping game of hide-and-seek, which produced great fun. But by far the most *recherché* scene of all was the bath.

You know that lovely lake, my Helen; for 'twas in its crystal water we first enjoyed love's blisses together.

In a few minutes we were all undressed and sportively splashing each other, swimming, kissing, tickling, fucking.

Oh, ye gods, what a scene it was. Such perfect abandon I do verily believe was never witnessed, even at Dionysian festivals of ancient Greece. But one thing was wanting to make us mad as the satyrs and bacchantes of those times. And that one thing I resolved to have – wine. I despatched Phoebe and Daphnis for a dozen of Burgundy. The cup circulated; we all became intoxicated; we performed prodigies of lust, gamahuched, and did everything that the most wanton imagination can conceive; so that coming at length out of the lake, in which some of the girls were near being drowned, none of the party save Cecilia, Mrs J., and myself could dress ourselves. Calling in the aid then of old Mrs Jukes, we first put Phoebe, Chloe, and Daphnis to bed. Then, huddling on the clothes of the other young ladies, we got them, as best we might, to the coach and sent them home at seven o'clock that summer's evening, as completely drunk as ever was a lady of pleasure in Covent Garden.

As for Cecilia and myself, we partook of a light supper, went to bed, and were soon in the arms of Morpheus.

To Livia

I find from my excellent friend, Mrs J., that she has given you an elaborate account of our late doings here, when we emulated the ancients with our Bacchanalian orgies. The finish of that scene was not, I must confess, at all to my taste, and we all suffered more or less the next day of our excess. I have therefore determined not to proceed to such lengths again.

Yesterday, being the breaking up for the holidays at Mrs J.'s, I proposed to her to invite the whole school of twenty-six young ladies. But not to injure the interests of the good lady, I promised that any little amorous fun that took place should be covert and accidental, apparently.

That if any of the innocent ones saw aught that might shock their notions of propriety, it should be so managed that they would never think it was a premeditated affront.

To this end I caused the statues of Priapus to be wreathed with laurel and ivy about the middle. I locked up all the naughty books and pictures, and as it was not intended to proceed to any voluptuous extremities while the young ladies were with us, I introduced on this occasion an excellent band of musicians, who were located in a tent pitched on a spot where they could observe little of the proceedings. From Ranelagh Gardens I brought Jackson, the fireworks man, at an expense of twenty pounds. During the morning he was very busy hanging variegated lamps on both sides of every verdant valley, and the taste he displayed was wonderful. The weather continued delicious, clear and warm, so it promised to be very effective. Meantime a sumptuous refection was prepared. The new and old swing were dusted and got ready, the fountains were set a playing, and when at three o'clock the young ladies arrived all was in readiness. Lady Cecilia looked charming in a white satin gown and quilted hoop of pink silk; her hair was delicately powdered, and Renaud, that prince of coiffeurs, had coquettishly placed a real rose on one side of her head, which had a vastly pretty effect. As for me I wore my grey tiffling coat, a pompadour waistcoat, grey satin breeches and silks, with my best pair of diamond buckles in my shoes. I also, in honour of my company, mounted my gold-hilted sword, mechlin lace ruffles, bag and solitaire.

Upon the arrival of the school we first of all discussed the viands set out on the grass under the shade of a wide-spreading elm. Six and twenty girls sitting on the lawn, you will readily suppose, could not all place themselves so correctly but what I got many a sly peep at legs, thighs, and cunnies I had never seen before; and the best of it was they were not the least aware of it, nor did the knowing ones – Mesdames Marshall, Jennings, Bellew, Augusta and Agnes – venture to give them a hint; so there I sat, eating the wing of a chicken and viewing the secret charms of four or five of the finest girls in the world.

The repast over, we proceeded to walk round the grounds, and when we came to the terminal figure of Priapus, the god of the garden, they all came to a halt; and while they considered him attentively, they asked me to explain all about his worship in ancient times, which I did to their entire satisfaction.

One tall, elegant girl of eighteen, Miss Medley, showed more curiosity than the others, and lingered behind to have a private view of the divinity. I had no doubt she wanted to see what it was the ivy concealed; so after we had got a little further I pretended that I had left my snuff box indoors, and deputing Cecilia to show them everything I stealthily returned and creeping up among the foliage at the back of the statue beheld the ivy removed and Miss Medley, on tiptoe, trying to rub her cunny against the marble Priape. Altering my position, therefore, so that she could see from my waist to my knees, but not my face, which the leaves concealed, I pulled out my own priape, which I handled till it was as big as the rural god's. She was some time before she saw it, but at length, when she did (supposing it was one of the musicians who was standing behind a tree for a necessary purpose), she recovered the statue, and placing herself behind it peeped out to see all that she could without being seen. Of course I shook the staff about and showed it off to the best advantage. She (not knowing I had seen her) displayed no alarm, nothing but intense curiosity; but I saw her right hand disappear under her clothes in a very mysterious manner; and from that moment I knew she was mine. With two strides I was beside her, finger on lip. She looked petrified with terror and shame, but I soon reassured her.

'My dear girl,' said I, 'this is what you want' (placing it in her hand), 'not the marble one, which is only to look at. Let me show you what use it is put to, and I promise not to tell Mrs J. anything I have seen.'

'Oh, pray, good sir, what would you do? Consider my honour, my virtue. Ah, my goodness, what will become of me?'

'Why, certainly,' said I, 'it would not be very pleasant for your mamma to be told how you have acted, and to look so long at a naked man when by quickly walking away, you would scarcely have seen him. Oh, fie, miss.'

'Oh, but, Sir Charles, you will not tell, will you?'

'Certainly not, if you comply with my wishes.'

And I clasped her firm posteriors with one hand and her beautiful glowing cunny with the other.

'But, Sir Charles, will it not hurt very much?'

'Well, it will hurt a little at first, but the pleasure will soon drown the pain.'

She was silent, but I felt her hand tremble as she squeezed my great prick between her taper white fingers.

That was enough, so lifting her in my arms I bore her to a little grove in which was a tool house never visited by anybody but the gardeners, and here putting a bundle of matting on a turned over wheelbarrow, I deposited the fair girl and was soon driving away at her maidenhead.

She bit her lip with the pain but did not cry out, which I considered a good omen; so caressingly slapping her thighs and handling her breasts and buttocks, I soon found a sensible moisture in that luscious part into which I was forcing my way – the darling girl was spending. Soon she gave tongue in delirious ejaculation: 'Ah! where am I? Oh! how nice it is. Ah – oh – bl – bliss! Ah, oh, ur – r – r – r!'

And grinding her teeth, she nearly squeezed the breath out of me, hugging me with her arms and entwining her thighs around my loins with a tiger-like strength that nearly broke my back.

This girl, who had large open blue eyes and a confident bold air, had evidently found what she had long required, only she did not know it, and that was a good stiff cock. And having found it, she had a good mind to keep it, for my crisis having come and desiring to withdraw, she would by no means let me, but planted her touches so wantonly and with such good effect that positively (a rare thing at my time of life) I got a second erection within ten minutes of the departure of the first.

She now grew quite bold and whispered me not to let it come so soon.

It consequently happened that we lingered half an hour in that delightful spot.

As soon as the beauteous Miss Medley had a little recovered herself, I raised her up and offering my arm went in search of her companions.

'Well?' said I, 'you find the real surpasses the *beau ideal*?'

'Not the same thing at all,' she whispered, pressing my arm.

'What pains me is the reflection that just as I have won, I am to lose you. You go home tomorrow, do you not?'

'Yes, that is so,' she said; then hesitating a little, she added, 'but if you really desire it, that need not prevent your seeing me, as I live no further than Richmond, and there are numerous lovely secluded spots where we could meet.'

I stopped involuntarily with surprise, then catching her up in my arms I covered her with kisses, exclaiming, 'Why, my angel, this is more than my fondest hopes could have suggested. Do you really mean what you say? Or, come now, acknowledge that you are laughing at me.'

'I, not the least in the world.'

'Then you really mean what you say.'

'*Ma foi*, yes; I find you a gallant man.'

I took off my hat and made a lower bow to Miss Medley than I ever made to a miss before.

Then renewing our conversation, she gave me full directions when I was to meet her, on what days, and at what hour. By the time she had finished we found ourselves in the midst of the merrymakers.

'Why, goodness gracious,' cried a dozen voices at once, 'where have you two been all this while? We had quite lost you both.'

Poor Miss Medley blushed, but I came to the rescue, quickly saying, 'You know, I went indoors for my snuff box; in returning I made a detour through the maze to see if the lamps had been hung to my mind and found Miss Medley, who had quite lost herself in its intricate winding and shouted to me to show her the way out, which after some time I was able to do, and here we are.'

This explanation satisfied the majority, but I saw Misses Marshall and Jennings exchange a meaning look, which I had no difficulty in reading, but of course took no notice.

We had interrupted a capital game at hide-and-seek, which was now continued.

It being Miss Jennings' turn to hide, away she tripped into the wood, but as she passed me she managed to squeeze a little crumpled billet, written in pencil, into my hand. As soon therefore as we heard 'whoop,' away we ran in every direction, and finding myself alone I seized the opportunity of reading it.

It was of a brevity perfectly Spartan: 'The tool house.'

To the tool house I therefore proceeded as fast as possible taking care none of the huntresses should see which way I took and pondering all the way on those two words.

Had it been Miss Marshall, all would have been clear enough, but what did the Jennings know about the tool house?

In the midst of my cogitations I saw it before me.

With a hasty glance to see that no one had followed me, I sprang over the threshold and shot the bolt behind me, and at that moment was clasped in the arms of the amorous girl.

'Oh, dear Sir Charles,' she exclaimed, 'this is kind of you, but you did awaken my passions, you know, and having aroused them, you will love me a little, will you not?'

'My darling girl,' I cried, kneeling at her feet and sliding my hands under her clothes, grasping her naked thighs, 'can you doubt it?'

'Well, yes, dear Sir Charles, I did doubt, for you are such a roué and such a votary to promiscuous love that I feared you might overlook poor little me, and now that bold Miss Medley with her great blue eyes has ensnared you, for you don't suppose your tale of the maze deceived me in the least –'

'Really,' said I, laughing.

'Oh, you are a terrible rake, Sir Charles.'

'You flatter me,' I said, with a low bow.

'And then,' cried the impetuous girl, as her dark eyes

flashed. 'I have to contend against the charms of Lady Cecilia, and Phoebe, and Chloe, and –'

'Stop, stop,' I exclaimed, 'and *halte la*! In these precincts sacred to Venus and Priapus the green-eyed monster jealousy is never allowed to intrude; my love extends to beauty wherever it is to be found, and like the bee I fly from flower to flower and extract the sweets from each; be satisfied then, my precious girl, with your own share, and you will, believe me, have no cause to complain.' And I imprinted a rapturous kiss on her damask cheek.

'But we are wasting precious moments in words, *ma petite*, let us proceed to deeds, if you please.'

And suiting the action to the word, I made her kneel upon the gardener's matting, which still remained on the wheelbarrow as I had left it, and tossing up her clothes exposed her voluptuous white hemispheres.

'Oh, my; good gracious,' cried the girl, 'is that the way it is done? I thought you would lie on my bosom.'

'There are various methods, my angel,' said I, beginning to push at the mark, 'and as we become better acquainted I hope to instruct you in the thirty-five positions.'

'*Juste ciel*!' ejaculated the pretty creature, 'are there so many, then?'

'Oh, yes,' I rejoined, 'and each more delightful than the other.'

And grasping her round the hips, I began to thrust in good earnest. She buckled to admirably, and merely giving a little 'oh!' of pain now and then, straddled and aided my entrance all she could, so that in about ten minutes I rode in at a canter, winning the race by a length.

Then, as she felt the swelling head of my stiffening weapon in the innermost depths of her cunny, this enamoured girl gave full vent of her delight. She jutted out her great white bottom, she passed her hand underneath and felt the balls of love; she manipulated me in a thousand ways, she bounded, wriggled, and twisted, sighed and cooed; her breath came short, and murmuring out, 'Ah, sweet bliss! Ah, it is Heaven! Heaven!' she spent; and my extatic movement, by a lucky chance coming at the same time, I sank forward on those white globes in a delirium of joy.

How long we should have lain thus, Venus only knows; but the sound of approaching footsteps roused us from our voluptuous trance. Hastily arranging my dress, I slipped out of the door and hid myself amongst the underwood. I had scarcely concealed myself when a bevy of girls appeared, shouting out at the top of their voices.

'Miss Jennings, Miss Jennings!'

'Where can she have hid herself?' cried one.

'I declare,' said another, 'I am quite hot and tired with looking for her.'

'I should not wonder if she is in this tool house,' cried another, 'let us see.'

And pushing open the door, they led her out, looking very confused and as red as a peony.

'Why, gracious goodness me, Miss Jennings, what could have induced you to choose such a place to hide?'

'Rather say,' answered the lovely girl, recovering her presence of mind, 'how foolish you all look at having been baffled so long.'

'Well, well, we have found you at last; so come along and let us have a game at hunt-the-slipper; we shall only just have time for one game before the fireworks, for see it is getting quite dark.' And the laughing girls led her off.

I was preparing to follow, not wishing to lose my share of a game I liked so well, when suddenly I felt a hand in mine, and turning looked down on the smiling, rosy face of Chloe.

'What! you here?' I cried, astonished. 'How's this?'

'Oh, don't be angry, your honour,' said she. 'I followed you and saw all that passed in the tool house through a chink in the door; but I will not tell.'

'Oh, you saucy little pussy,' I cried, patting her rosy

cheek, 'and what do you want of me now?'

'Ah, Sir Charles, that you must guess, you know.'

'Egad,' said I, 'that I can discern quite well, you funny little thing; but tell me, do you then like to have me, better than young Daphnis. He, so young, so beautiful, so near your own age, I so old compared to yourself. Is this possible?'

'Why, to tell you the truth, Sir Charles, I have a stronger liking for you than for him. He is too pretty by half, too like a girl; besides you taught me all I know of love; you first awakened those feelings; it was your hand first caressed that secret part which now always thrills when I approach you. Oh, Sir Charles, young as I am, I have all a woman's feelings.'

'Then, my dear love, you shall have all a woman's pleasure. Come,' and I led her into the wood, and laying on my back made her get over me.

'I am rather tired, my love,' said I, 'so you must do all the work.'

'That I will, and with pleasure, dear Sir Charles; but oh, dear me, you are not stiff, hardly at all; but I will soon remedy that. Let me gamahuche you; and if you like, do you gamahuche me and then we shall soon be ready.'

So saying, she turned round, presenting her lovely bottom and pressing her cunny to my lips, my tongue slipped in at once, while she, taking my languid prick in her rosy mouth, so skilfully titillated it that in a very few minutes I was ready for action.

Again, therefore, reversing her attitude, she mounted me and a delightful fuck ensued.

The whole affair did not occupy a quarter of an hour, And this little act in the drama being concluded, we joined the revels.

I will not weary you with a recapitulation of all the frolic of hunt-the-slipper; suffice it to say that without any apparent offence against propriety, I managed to accidentally, as it were, feel many a virgin cunny and many a plump thigh that night.

The fête concluded with a country dance amidst a general illumination and superb display of fireworks. Supper was then served and my guests departed about twelve, much delighted with their visit.

When they were gone and Cecilia and I had retired to bed, we compared notes of our various adventures.

She, it appeared, had not been idle, and attaching herself to Daphnis and Miss Bellew, they retreated to the grotto where fucking and gamahuching occupied them for an hour. She had also much diverted herself with pretty Clara, to whom she had privately shown the ponies, and after exciting the young woman with the sight and by lascivious touches, had finally gamahuched her and been gamahuched to their mutual satisfaction.

She laughed heartily at the conquest I had made of Miss Medley's heart and asked if I intended to go to Richmond?

I fancied there was rather more eagerness than usual in her manner, and as I knew her not to be troubled with jealousy, I could not quite understand it. But dissembling my surprise, I answered, coolly, 'Why, yes, I suppose I must go. That girl is quite a Messalina and would never forgive me if I disappointed her.'

'Is it possible,' said Cecilia, 'her bold blue eyes meant something then?'

'Indeed they did,' I rejoined, 'and let me tell you, she is an uncommon fine girl, and quite ripe.'

Nothing more passed, and after a little languid toying, for we were both tired out, we fell asleep.

The following Monday was the day appointed for me to go to Richmond, but all the way, as I rode along, I felt a vague uneasiness about Cecilia which I could not account for. There was a feverish excitement of manner about her the last few days. She was absent and abstracted, gave incoherent answers, or none at all, and was altogether quite unlike herself. What could it mean? I asked myself again and again, but at length, weary of speculation, I put spurs to my horse and galloped on.

Arrived at Richmond, I put up my horse at the Star and Garter, and enquiring my way to the Rectory (as a blind) I strolled slowly on; by and by I came to the wood which Miss Medley had so carefully described to me, and following a particular path I soon arrived at the trysting place.

Imagine my surprise when, instead of my lovely friend, I found an old gipsy woman seated under the tree. On seeing me, she rose, and dropping me a curtsey handed me a little three cornered and scented billet. I tore it open, and read these words.

'I have not been sufficiently careful with my linen; some stains have been seen and my aunt will not let me go out alone – I am in despair.'

I put half-a-crown into the old woman's hand and turned on my heel. She stopped me.

'What, your honour, are you going away without an effort? Consider, sir, the young lady is over head and ears in love with you; leave the matter to me, and I will arrange it.'

'Say you so, my good woman,' said I, 'in that case I will pay you well. You know who I am, I suppose?'

'Of course I do, your honour, all our tribe know you well, Sir Charles, for have you ever turned us off your land; have you ever taken us before the beak when we robbed your poultry yard; do you not let us sleep in your barns; and did you not send us camp blankets and provisions last winter? Oh, we know you very well, and a right noble gentleman you are. A little given to the girls, perhaps, like other fine gentlemen, but what of that? Now look you, Sir Charles, we gipsies have a mysterious way of finding out things – take a friendly hint, don't return the same way you came, go the other road, or blood may come of it.'

So saying, and before I could prevent her, she dived into the wood and disappeared.

The plot thickened and I began to feel now really uncomfortable, but you know cowardice was never one of my faults; besides I had my sword, not the toy called by the name which one wears on gala occasions but a plain, strong, serviceable weapon which had served me well in several duels; I therefore rode on the way I came, regardless of the gipsy's caution.

As I rode along the road which traverses the wood skirting my demesne, I observed a coach with imperial and portmanteaus strapped upon it, drawn up as if for concealment off the road, and almost hidden amongst the trees. The coachman lay stretched on the grass while the horses grazed as they stood.

Taking no further notice of this travelling equipage I rode into the wood, and tying my horse to a tree wandered about in different directions. At length, about fifty yards from me in a small open glade, I could perceive through the trees a lady and gentleman in amorous dalliance. I approached stealthily without being seen and ensconced myself in a copse, where I had full view of all that passed, though I could not hear what was said.

On the grass lay a tall handsome dark man, who I at once recognised as Lady Cecilia's cousin, Lord William B., while lying upon the young man was her ladyship herself, her clothes thrown up, displaying all her hinder beauties which Lord B., was playfully slapping as she bounded up and down upon him.

They were evidently very much pleased with each other, and the rapturous kisses, the 'oh!' and 'ahs!' were the only sounds that reached me. After some time they reversed the position, he kneeling up behind her and she wriggling and bounding in the most extatic delight.

At length, their climax came. She turned round and throwing her arms round her lover's neck, they sank down quite exhausted.

In an age when the spirit of amorous intrigue pervades the court, it was not to be expected that a person of quality like Lady Cecilia would be very rigid, more especially as Lord

William B., was an old flame of hers.

And remembering my own infidelities towards her I should never have taken umbrage at any she might have indulged in, had they been carried on openly as mine were. But this clandestine meeting when she thought I was gone out for the day disturbed me.

I was anxious to gather from their conversation what was the meaning of it. So soon, therefore, as they finished their first delights and were seated lovingly side by side on the grass, I crept up through the gorse and underwood till I found myself about a yard from them. Here, motionless as a statue, my hand on my sword, I listened.

'I was saying,' said Lord William, 'that this man must be a thorough old beast, a goat, a satyr, my dear coz, who ought never to have had you. The things you have told me, and pardi, I am no saint, really quite make my hair stand on end. Fie, fie –'

'Perhaps,' cried Cecilia, laughing, 'he would say could he hear you, to amuse oneself with young women is one thing, but to debauch another man's wife is another. Damme, fie, fie –'

Lord William laughed; but bit his lip, annoyed at the repartee.

'In fine, my dear William,' said Cecilia, 'it is so much easier to see the wickedness of other people's actions than our own. I'll venture to assert that if every man now living got his deserts, there would be few escape. Let fanatics abuse their fellow creatures, condemning them wholesale to hell – human nature, depend upon it, is the same everywhere under a parson's cassock or soldier's scarlet coat.'

'Granted, my little philosopher,' laughed her cousin, 'but did you not tell me that you regarded your husband with abhorrence and detestation?'

'Oh, doubtless, doubtless! Yes, he is detestable; a horrid, debauched old scoundrel, no question; but that is no reason you, who have just made him a cuckold, should add insult to

161

injury by calling him names. How do you know that he is not nearer than we think and might suddenly –'

'Appear!' I hoarsely exclaimed springing into the open space where they were seated, sword in hand.

'To your feet, my lord; draw and defend yourself. The intrigue I could have pardoned, for it is the custom of the age in which we live; but the abuse is too insulting, and on your part, my lady, too cruel; but enough of words. Guard!'

I placed myself in fencing attitude. Lord William (who was an antagonist not to be despised, being one of the first swordsmen of the day), raised his sword to his head *en salute*; then gracefully throwing himself into the second position our blades crossed with a clashing sound that elicited a little shriek from Lady Cecilia, who sank, half fainting on the greensward.

The duel lasted some time; we were combatants worthy of each other. *Carte* and *tierce, volte,* and *demi volte,* all the finesse of fencing was tried by each for some time in vain.

At length I pricked him in the sword arm and his cambric sleeve was crimsoned in an instant. The wound only roused his anger; he lost his coolness and did not keep himself so well covered; lunging then under his *tierce* guard, I should certainly have despatched him had not the traitress, Lady Cecilia, at that instant struck up my arm with Lord William's cane; and at the same moment his sword passed through my body.

I fell back like a dead man, without sense or motion.

When I again opened my eyes, they rested on various familiar objects; I was in my private chamber. At the foot of the bed was seated Phoebe, he eyes red with weeping. I tried to speak, but she put her finger to her lip, and approaching, said, 'Pray don't try yet, Sir Charles.'

'What has happened?' I faintly exclaimed.

'Not now, not now,' whispered Phoebe; 'you shall know all about it another time. You have been lightheaded and very ill, and for three days that kind young surgeon who scarcely ever left your side despaired of your life; but if you will only keep quiet, dear Sir Charles, all may yet be well.'

She put a cooling drink to my lips, and shading the light moved further off. I found myself from loss of blood to be weak as a baby, so closing my eyes was soon again unconscious. In another week I was a little better, to the great delight of the poor doctor (to whom I had certainly shown many acts of kindness, never expecting such a faithful and grateful return for it). He told me that the right lung had been pierced and that the haemorrhage had at first been so great that he despaired of staunching it; but that quiet, the excellent nursing of old Jukes, Phoebe, and Chloe, who had sat up with me in turns, and an iron constitution had combined to save me. He said not a word of himself or his own skill, so that when, about a month afterwards, being convalescent, I presented him with a cheque for one hundred guineas, he regarded me with astonishment, declaring that ten was all he deserved; but I would not be gainsaid and sent him away rejoicing.

Feeling myself well enough to hear Phoebe's recital, and kissing her and Chloe and even poor old Jukes with much ardour as I thanked them for their tender care of me, I made the two former seat themselves, at my feet, while Daphnis placed a pillow at my back and handed me a glass of lemonade.

'It is little I have to tell you, Sir Charles,' began Phoebe, 'but I will endeavour to be as clear as possible. Soon after your departure for Richmond, her ladyship went out alone on foot. As we had no orders to watch my lady, I would not permit Jack to do so, and we saw her no more. About five in the afternoon Jack was rambling about in the woods outside the walls when suddenly he came upon the spot where, to his great horror, you lay weltering in your blood.

'There was blood on the turf all about, which was much trampled down. You lay on you back, pale as death. Near you he picked up a fan, a ribbon, and a lady's glove; and returning to the dairy at speed he at once told us what had happened, directed us to bring your body in quietly and make up a bed in this room while he galloped off for the doctor.'

'My dear boy,' said I, extending him my hand, 'your presence of mind and decision in all probability saved my life. I thank you, and will remember it. Go on, Phoebe.'

'Well, sir, we did just as he bid us, and the doctor came; you know the rest.'

'And Lady Cecilia?' I exclaimed.

'Oh,' said Phoebe, 'Jack must tell you about her ladyship, for as soon as he had heard what the doctor had to say and saw you in good hands, he brought your horse, which you had left tied to a tree, into the yard, put a pair of loaded pistols into the holsters, buckled on your short sword and rode away.'

'Do you, then, continue the narrative, Daphnis,' said I.

The boy hesitated a moment, and then began.

'You will readily understand, Sir Charles, that being quick of apprehension, seeing you lying there with your drawn sword still in your hand, a glove, a ribbon, a fan, and the prints of strange foot marks, and those, too, from shoes not such as are generally worn by the vulgar or by highwaymen, I rapidly came to the conclusion that my lady had met a gallant in the wood, that you had surprised them, and that the duel was the consequence.

'Then I followed the footprints in the moist mossy turf, which showed clear owing to the recent rains, until they nearly reached the road; here the marks of wheels appeared, a coach-and-four had been driven off the road and into the wood, had stopped where the footprints ended, and then skirting the wood, debouched on the road. Putting spurs to your horse's flanks, I galloped on. At the next town I heard news of the fugitives; twelve miles further on they had changed horses; at the next six miles they had supped. It was now quite dark, but still I galloped on; soon however I lost them; there were three roads in diverse directions and no one could give me a clue to the one they had taken. Horse and self being now quite worn out, I stopped at the nearest inn and retired to rest. The next morning I made the best of my way to Hastings. Here I learnt that a lady and gentleman answering their description had sailed for France five hours before.'

I thanked Daphnis for his zeal, but assured him he had taken a great deal of unnecessary trouble.

I will now conclude this long story by telling you I subsequently heard that Lord William having quarrelled with a Frenchman at a public gaming table, blows ensued which resulted in a duel, and the Frenchman left his lordship stark dead on the field.

As for Lady Cecilia, broken hearted at the loss of her cousin and lover, she entered a convent of Benedictine nuns and has lately taken the black veil.

But it is time to put an end to this long letter, so, adieu!

Conclusion

To Thalia

You ask me, dear friend, where I have been hiding myself the last fifteen years. Alas! we are both that much older since we last corresponded. I was, however, about to indite a letter to you, having heard from Jack Bellsize that you had just returned from India with your husband, the General.

You duly received my communication of the affair with Lord William B., you tell me, and wrote a long letter in reply, but I never got it.

After these unfortunate events, I took a disgust to my villa at Twickenham, which I sold for a good price to Sir Bulkeley H., and retreated, with Pheobe, Chloe, Daphnis and old Jukes, to my Hertfordshire estate, where I have resided ever since.

As for Miss Medley, having heard from the gipsy of my intended departure she eloped one night from her aunt's and joined us. She remained with me about five years when an opportunity offering for her to make an advantageous marriage with a young farmer, I persuaded her to have him and stocked their farm for them.

To Mrs J., I presented the house in which she lived, taking an affectionate farewell of that excellent lady. Augusta and Agnes I suitably provided for, and also found husbands for Miss Marshall and Miss Jennings, giving to each a dowry.

Poor old Jukes died five years since, come Michaelmas.

Daphnis I started in life with an ensign's commission in a marching regiment when he was about eighteen; poor lad, he fell gloriously while leading his men at a forlorn hope in storming some place in the Low Countries (not Cunnyland), such is the fortune of war; and a more gallant youth never campaigned in the fields of Venus or Mars.

Phoebe, now a fine buxom woman of thirty-five, retains all her good looks and much of her freshness. She is sweet tempered and affectionate as ever.

Chloe too has grown up a lovely creature.

Having 'lived every day of my life,' as the saying is, you will readily suppose that I cannot perform the feats of Venus I once indulged in, but two or three blooming girls who pass for the sisters and cousins of Phoebe and Chloe serve to amuse me by their playfullness and tumbling about, showing their beauties, sometimes stir my sluggish blood into a thrill.

Occasionally I am able to remind Phoebe and Chloe of my old vigour and have a fucktious romp, but – 'From fifty to four-score, once a week and no more.'

They each have a strapping young fellow as a lover, and my consideration in this regard, so far from alienating them, only makes them more amiable and compliant to my wishes.

By my neighbours these dear girls and old friends are regarded as favourite domestics merely, a discreet old woman, the cook, who supplied old Jukes' place, playing propriety. So I am no longer a rake.

The rector of the parish is my very good friend.

My faithful surgeon lives in the house, being still a bachelor.

So, with the extra aid of two neighbouring squires, we have our bowl of punch and a rubber.

This quiet life suits me admirably, and I have forever bid adieu tō the gay world and the pleasures of the town; passing much of my time in reading those philosophical writers, who are just now making such an impression on the public mind.

And now, dear friend having given you all the news, I

would fain express a hope that you will some day find your way into this remote region, but if the fates decree otherwise, then accept my farewell. *Vale! Vale! Longum Vale!*

ADULT READS

ANONYMOUS AUTHORS

0352314850	**The Adventures of a Schoolboy**	£2.50
0352313269	**Beatrice**	£2.99*
0352314915	**The Boudoir**	£2.99*
0352317884	**Confessions of an English Maid**	£2.75*
0352322152	**The Devils Advocate**	£2.99
0352317221	**Eroticon**	£2.99
0352318627	**Eroticon II**	£2.99
0352321660	**Eroticon III**	£2.99
0352313374	**Eveline**	£2.99*

These books are obtainable from many booksellers and newsagents. If you have any difficulty tick the titles you want and fill in the form below.

Name _____

Address _____

_____

Send to: Nexus Cash Sales, P.O. Box 11, Falmouth, Cornwall, TR10 9EN.

Please send a cheque or postal order to the value of the cover price plus: UK: 55p for the first book, 22p for the second book and 14p for each additional book ordered to the maximum charge of £1.75.

BFPO and EIRE: 55p for the first book, 22p for the second book, 14p per copy for the next 7 books, thereafter 8p per book.

OVERSEAS: £1.00 for the first book and 25p per copy for each additional book.

While every effort is made to keep prices low, it is sometimes necessary to increase prices at short notice. Nexus reserve the right to show new retail prices on covers which may differ from those advertised in the text or elsewhere.

*NOT FOR SALE IN CANADA

ADULT READS

0352312327	The Romance of Lust Book I	£2.99*
035231267X	The Romance of Lust Book II	£2.99*
035231544X	Rosa Fielding	£2.25*
0352311312	Suburban Souls Book I	£2.25*
0352311762	Suburban Souls Book II	£2.50*
0352314605	Three Times A Woman	£2.99*
0352317809	Violette	£2.50
0352317299	The Fiesta Letters	£2.50
0352316438	The Fiesta Book of Saucy Crosswords	£1.95
035231852X	JANE ANNE ROBERTS The Secret Web	£2.50

These books are obtainable from many booksellers and newsagents. If you have any difficulty tick the titles you want and fill in the form below.

Name _____

Address _____

_____

Send to: Nexus Cash Sales, P.O. Box 11, Falmouth, Cornwall, TR10 9EN.

Please send a cheque or postal order to the value of the cover price plus: UK: 55p for the first book, 22p for the second book and 14p for each additional book ordered to the maximum charge of £1.75.

BFPO and EIRE: 55p for the first book, 22p for the second book, 14p per copy for the next 7 books, thereafter 8p per book.

OVERSEAS: £1.00 for the first book and 25p per copy for each additional book.

While every effort is made to keep prices low, it is sometimes necessary to increase prices at short notice. Nexus reserve the right to show new retail prices on covers which may differ from those advertised in the text or elsewhere.

*NOT FOR SALE IN CANADA

ADULT READS

0352313781	**A Man With a Maid Vol III**	£2.99*
0352316209	**Maudie**	£2.25
0352314826	**The Memoirs of Dolly Morton**	£2.25
0352313692	**More Eveline**	£2.99*
0352318457	**A Night in a Moorish Harem**	£2.50*
0352311355	**Oh Wicked Country!**	£2.25
0352316756	**Parisian Frolics**	£2.25*
0352320494	**Pleasure Bound**	£2.95
0352315687	**Randiana**	£2.99*

These books are obtainable from many booksellers and newsagents. If you have any difficulty tick the titles you want and fill in the form below.

Name _____

Address _____

_____

Send to: Nexus Cash Sales, P.O. Box 11, Falmouth, Cornwall, TR10 9EN.

Please send a cheque or postal order to the value of the cover price plus:
UK: 55p for the first book, 22p for the second book and 14p for each additional book ordered to the maximum charge of £1.75.

BFPO and EIRE: 55p for the first book, 22p for the second book, 14p per copy for the next 7 books, thereafter 8p per book.

OVERSEAS: £1.00 for the first book and 25p per copy for each additional book.

While every effort is made to keep prices low, it is sometimes necessary to increase prices at short notice. Nexus reserve the right to show new retail prices on covers which may differ from those advertised in the text or elsewhere.

NOT FOR SALE IN CANADA

ADULT READS

035232063X	CELESTE ARDEN **Dreams of Fair Women**	£2.50
0352315164	ALAIN DORVAL **Indiscreet Memoires**	£2.95
035232046X	ANTHONY GREY **A Gallery of Nudes**	£2.95*
0352320575	MARCUS VAN HELLER **Roman Orgy**	£2.95*
0352318724	E.K. **Regine**	£2.75*
0352304200	SARAH KERNOCHAN **Dry Hustle**	£2.95*
0352317353	LAURE-ANNE **Laure-Anne**	£2.25

These books are obtainable from many booksellers and newsagents. If you have any difficulty tick the titles you want and fill in the form below.

Name _____

Address _____

_____

Send to: Nexus Cash Sales, P.O. Box 11, Falmouth, Cornwall, TR10 9EN.

Please send a cheque or postal order to the value of the cover price plus:
UK: 55p for the first book, 22p for the second book and 14p for each additional book ordered to the maximum charge of £1.75.

BFPO and EIRE: 55p for the first book, 22p for the second book, 14p per copy for the next 7 books, thereafter 8p per book.

OVERSEAS: £1.00 for the first book and 25p per copy for each additional book.

While every effort is made to keep prices low, it is sometimes necessary to increase prices at short notice. Nexus reserve the right to show new retail prices on covers which may differ from those advertised in the text or elsewhere.

*NOT FOR SALE IN CANADA